THE MOLYBDUS ARTICULATE

SHANE HAWKS

THE BIZARCHIVES

The Bizarchives
Weird Tales of Monsters, Magic, and Machines

Presented by

The Midgard Institute
of Science Fiction & Fantasy Literature

To my daughter, Lydia.
May the stars always raise more questions than they answer. You will forever be my masterpiece.

FOREWORD

Cosmic horror as a cohesive, defined form of literature has existed for over a hundred years now but typically as a niche genre read by the sensitive few individuals around the world (to paraphrase the titan of terror H.P. Lovecraft's tale The Call of Cthulhu). Such a designation is perhaps unfairly misleading and may give an impression that it is a genre lacking greatness which cannot be further from reality. I would in fact call it the most intense genre of horror there is, for there is no happy ending for humanity to be found here.

The idea of cosmic horror as a form of literature typically started around the late 19th century, the age of Ambrose Bierce, Algernon Blackwood, Arthur Machen, Robert W. Chambers, and others, and saw horror displayed to readers in a shocking new way. Gone were the typical horrors of old such as the duality of good against evil and presented new were horrors which cannot always be conceived, seen, touched, or most tragically, defeated. Human beings are left at the mercy of forces beyond understanding and as a result often came death, insanity, the twisting of the human mind and the perversion of the physical form in ways most unsavory.

The master of this genre came later, having learned to refine the works of the previously mentioned progenitors of the genre: Howard Phillips Lovecraft. So great was his influence on horror, so well did he refine the genre that cosmic horror quickly became known as Lovecraftian horror. To this day the terms cosmic and Lovecraftian horror are used interchangeably. It is from him that almost all subsequent writers took influence, even the great contemporary pulp writers such as Clark Ashton Smith and Robert E. Howard who wrote tales in tribute to their friend, Lovecraft. Many writers from around the world found an ancient and bizarre meaning in his tales and began to write their own, either pastiches or completely fresh, unrelated tales which took the core ideas of the Lovecraftian horror (or cosmic horror if you like) and saw the writer twist his or her imagination into newer directions.

With Shane Hawks' finely written Molybdus Articulate we see here the continuation of the fine tradition of the previously mentioned sensitive few around the world who were moved by not only the masters of old but also that sense of dread one feels for existence and that realization that horrific, nameless forces are under the veil of reality. A horror which makes any vampire, demon, or ghost pale in comparison. The Molybdus Articulate sees our protagonist, a hardy detective, take on a case that leads him to a secretive yet all but mundane town where he is faced with something that is best left undisturbed...

Hawks' tale follows some of the cornerstones of the genre in a style that shows his grasp of the genre, cornerstones which I know that are only ever a welcomed site by readers of Lovecraftian horror. Where Hawks' makes his deviations from the expected steps in such a tale there are only fresh and intriguing surprises which creates a tale which is no pastiche but an interesting new branch of the genre.

This is a vital point when it comes to writers of Lovecraftian horror. It's no doubt that though many writers wish to write in this genre, it is simply not something that can just be superficially emulated, nor taken lightly. One cannot simply add tentacles the way one might simply add fangs to a vampire tale and Mr. Hawks' grasp of the genre is solid and expressed through a writing style that fans of H.P. Lovecraft will be quite at home with.

I look forward to anything more coming from the mind of Mr. Hawks, a figure to watch out for in the 21st century era of Lovecraftian horror.

Damien Zehnder – Arkham Reporter

CONTENTS

My name is Edmond Jameson and I will recall for you now a tale I am certain you will not understand, but if I do not purge it from the turbulent recesses of my precarious mind it will spread its inky malignance and consume all of me.

PART I - THE JOURNAL

The year is 1934 and five days ago I was a private investigator. It was a mostly mundane job, brimming with surveillance and a not inconsiderable amount of research. The majority of my cases were simple enough; tail a husband to determine if he's having an affair, track down a son or estranged parent and so on. The work was fairly easy and the pay fulfilled my minimalist needs well enough.

In the fall of that year a queer fellow reached out to me by the name of Benjamin Hammond with an assignment that, at first, struck me as nothing unusual. I was to track down and retrieve an item, alluded to in a peculiar journal purchased at an estate sale a number of years prior. Now, I feel I must be rather insistent about the strange nature of this gentleman. When first I laid eyes on him, upon him answering the door, a great sense of unease washed over me for reasons I was not able to rationalize into coherent thought. He was kind enough in a professional sort of way and his attire didn't stray too far beyond what was expected but still... there was a kind of sallowness about his waxy complexion that I found to be unnerving.

That in conjunction with his decidedly tall and gaunt structure made for a bizarre sight. When I greeted him with a handshake I must admit that I had to stifle a shiver as his palms were uncomfortably cool and damp. As our eyes met I noticed that his were unremarkable save for the jaundiced yellow coloration of the whites. He invited me inside and kindly ushered me into a quaint parlor off the main hallway where he showed me to a tall and rather ostentatious wingback chair. I sat and he took the adjacent seat. He spoke in an accent I was unfamiliar with and the cadence of his speech was slow, deliberate and somewhat disjointed.

"I thank you for taking the time out of your busy schedule to meet with me, Mr. Jameson. I must confess I was beginning to fear I'd never find someone competent enough for this assignment."

The man smiled kindly but as his lips parted I caught a glimpse of the teeth within. Short and tiny little things crammed into neat rows, as if this man had not only never lost his milk teeth as a child but had in fact acquired many more over the course of his lifetime. Far too many teeth, I thought, but at such a cursory glance I couldn't say for certain with any degree of conviction.

I smiled in turn, combating my inner revulsion as I replied. "Please, call me Edmond. I never was one for formalities. It's nice to make your acquaintance, Mr. Hammond. You reached out to me at quite an opportune time, as I had just put to rest my most recent case. Tragic, that one. Nevertheless, my busy schedule, as you put it, is not as busy as you'd imagine. It's fortunate that you phoned when you did."

This, of course, was not wholly the truth but I've found that it instills a sense of confidence in the client when they believe their case is the sole case on my workload. It wasn't wholly a lie either as I have several open cases as of yet unsolved but the majority of these have reached dead ends and this assignment seemed simple enough.

. . .

"Now, Mr. Hammond. When we spoke on the phone you'd mentioned a certain item of interest described within a journal, is that correct?"

I removed my worn leather notebook from the inner pocket of my coat and readied myself to write down as many details as possible.

"Yes, that is correct. Well, mostly. You see, the item in question is never quite specified. I attended an estate sale roughly 3 years ago in Gloucester. The estate itself was a majestic Victorian piece of architecture that had tragically fallen into disrepair. The elderly gentleman that owned the property had recently passed. From what I cannot say although I recall mention of his infirmity being the result of his faculties steady and persistent decline. I left with a few items that drew my attention, a tempestuous oil painting, a marble bust depicting the likeness of Hippocrates, a wonderfully detailed tapestry portraying an artistic interpretation of the Wild Hunt, and of course, one queer leather bound journal.

In hindsight I couldn't tell you just why I wanted the accursed thing. Curiosity, I suppose. Its worn and terribly damaged, with water stains and mold, the brass adornments tarnished and altogether filthy. There are entire pages therein that are simply indecipherable largely due to the degree of damage they've sustained. I can only assume that the journal was penned by the estate owner, although there is at no point any mention as to who the scribe is. The specific item in question remains tantalizingly shrouded in mystery. Its physicality is briefly described as "prismatic, opalescent and irregular in both pattern and structure" but curiously throughout the entirety of the journal no further mention of the item's description is made, although it is often alluded to.

. . .

THE SENSATIONS that the item evokes, on the other hand, are prominent in the texts. I'm certain that you'll understand once you've perused the contents for yourself, Mr. Jameson."

He punctuated this final statement with a knowing if not distant gaze and the slight upturn at the corner of his lips conveyed the impression of amusement, and yet for reasons I could not place I was left with a sinister chill slowly edging it's way deeper into my sound senses.

"How intriguing." I said absentmindedly. "Now, obviously this is no business of my own but I wonder if you wouldn't indulge me nonetheless, Mr. Hammond. What would a reputable man like yourself want with such a decidedly peculiar object?"

The vacant yellow eyes of Benjamin Hammond focused upon me once more and he seemed to ponder my inquiry for some time before deeming to reply,

"Why, I am an artist of course." He said, gesturing around him at several canvas paintings upon the walls.

I must admit that prior to that moment I hadn't paid them any mind or particular interest for that matter but now that my eye had been drawn towards them I couldn't help but admire this otherwise irredeemable man's skill with a paintbrush.

He continued, "I learned to paint before I learned to walk. That's what my mother would have told you. The truth is that art, like most anything, takes patience and practice to master. I've been at it for all but 50 years and I'm afraid I'm only halfway there. The problem, though, with things that take great time is that once you've finally perfected that thing the world has moved on to another. A good artist has skill but a successful artist has foresight. I used to know what the world wanted, how to express myself in such a way that the world would receive my paintings with resounding applause. I have since learned that foresight is finite and will falter in time.

I want the object because I believe it to be an untapped muse, a font of inspiration and a window into the heart of modern man. I know how that must sound to someone such as yourself, someone governed by logic and reason. Again, you will understand soon enough, Edmond."

He spoke my name with such familiarity, such informal intimacy that I was momentarily caught off guard, forgetting that I had requested he call me by my given name.

"Excuse me for a moment and I will retrieve the journal for you."

With a slight groan Hammond stood from his seat and strode across the hardwood floor, through the doorway and down the hallway, presumably to a study or perhaps a library or any such room where one would expect to find literature.

I sank deeper into the plush crushed velvet cushions of my chair and admired the nearest of the aforementioned paintings. A scene static in time, a turbulent sea of roaring vengeful whitecaps mercilessly buffeting the feeble hull of a merchant vessel, pummeled nearly to capsizing. Hammond masterly captured the menacingly frightening scale of the unconquerable ocean and the insignificance of the vessel in contrast. The entire piece evoked such a feeling of hopeless terror, of frailty and helplessness that for the briefest of moments I could have sworn I was there, swaying upon the slick deck of that ship waiting to be devoured by the bottomless black maw churning and roiling beneath the hull.

So lost was I in that painting that I hadn't heard Hammond return and when he entered my periphery he gave me quite the start. Having noticed my sudden alarm he quickly said with a disarming chuckle,

"Do forgive me. I dare say there isn't enough weight upon these old bones to make much in the way of audible footsteps these days. I hope I didn't startle you too much?"

. . .

"Not at all, Mr. Hammond. The fact that you startled me at all is a testament to your talent. I was quite taken with this piece." I replied, gesturing to the painting.

"Ah yes, 'The Maelstrom' is the title of this particular painting. I was so pleased with the end result that I decided to keep it in my personal collection. It's not often that an artist is satisfied with their own work and as such it is invaluable to me. I painted it shortly after my late wife's passing and it has proved to be rather cathartic. I'm pleased to know that its impression is not lost on you."

As he approached I stood from my chair with a soft groan of my own, feeling the small fragments of shrapnel grating in my hip. Hammond extended one gangly arm in my direction and held between his spindly fingers a small brown journal, bound in leather. The pages within were swollen and stained, the binding broken and abused. The leather itself was aged and worn, bearing years of marring scars. Upon the corners, save for one that appears to have fallen off at some point, there were brass caps worn brown with time and that had accrued a greenish patina in certain places. Debossed in the center of the leather cover was some kind of mark or sigil consisting of a few harsh angular lines that tore across one another in a jagged pattern that vaguely resembled a trident.

That symbol made my stomach quiver and palms sweat and I was hesitant to accept the journal from this strange client, with his strange job and strange appearance and for a second I considered simply turning around and fleeing as quickly as I could manage.

. . .

SWALLOWING the sour bile inexplicably rising in the recesses of my throat I tentatively reached out and grasped the cool leather journal.

My eyes met Mr. Hammonds and I said, "Excellent. I'll begin my research immediately and, with any luck, I'll be on my way to retrieve this item in a day or so. I'll be in touch." Truth be told I couldn't have ended this exchange soon enough and I was eager to be done with it. A nausea had crept into me and I was suddenly quite sensitive to the light. Our business having been concluded I bid Hammond farewell and took my leave, clasping the journal tightly in my hands.

Some festering and malignant malaise had overtaken me upon laying eyes on that eerie sigil and it took what little remained of my dwindling fortitude to make it safely home. Once there I lurched through the front door, feverishly scrambling towards the bathroom where I practically threw myself headlong at the porcelain toilet bowl before violently retching up the contents of the meager lunch I'd eaten earlier.

After dry heaving at irregular intervals for a few more agonizing minutes I cleaned up and carried myself to my bedchamber. I drew the shades and immediately collapsed into bed, falling into a deep and dreamless sleep.

I woke horribly disoriented in darkness, fumbling to turn on the bedside lamp. I had slept well into the night it seemed but still, I was feeling rejuvenated and so I rose, prepared a cup of cold coffee leftover from that morning and made my way to the study with Hammond's journal in hand. I crossed the room to my desk, took a seat and stared at the journal before me. Putting the silly superstitions out of my mind I opened the cover and began reading.

· · ·

To say that the contents therein were eccentric would be a colossal understatement. It started innocuously enough, the thoughts of a middle aged man with depression living a lonely life and working a job that was going nowhere as a traveling salesman. He mentioned a son that had perished in the war like so many others, a wife that left him after their son's death and a great inner void that remained in their absence.

The author mentioned several specific townships and boroughs he'd traveled to for his employer; Essex, Falmouth, Chatham and so on. He'd note certain lodgings he particularly enjoyed, memorable landmarks, the occasional person that had made a lasting impression. All mundane and fairly droll, but then, roughly two-thirds into the stained and pulpy pages, things took a perplexing turn. The author spoke of traveling to a town by the name of Ellsworth to peddle his wares. There is a certain passage that read:

'As I was drawing near to Ellsworth I spied a quaint seaside village nestled against the cliffside bluffs. It seems to me to be most picturesque. I believe I will visit this small town after my business here is through and perhaps take in the scenery for an evening before continuing on my way.'"

THE NEXT ENTRY in the journal was of a drastically different timbre:

'I ARRIVED HERE THIS MORNING. I'm certain of it, but if that's the case then why is there several days worth of growth on my face? I shaved the night before departing Concord. No, not Concord. Newport? Good lord, where was I? I'm feeling a little backwards. I arrived this morning, had a bite to eat at a local restaurant and then went down to the shore for a walk. All easy enough to recall. After that I cannot remember. I'm so hungry.'

FROM THERE THE entries descended into a spiral of uncanny fixation, infatuation and obsession. What followed was the author's steady decline into certain madness.

'I RETURNED to the shore in the hopes of retracing my steps and found myself drawn to the lighthouse. I was taken with a familiar sense of déjà vu as I approached the towering structure and when I reached the base I was surprised to see the door ajar. I entered with a boyish sense of mischief tingling in my belly, knowing I shouldn't be there but urged onward by some unspoken need for closure. Ascending the steep spiral staircase within I had to stop several times to catch my breath but with each step the need to reach the top grew more insistent. I passed through many a strange chamber as I climbed higher but by the time I arrived at the pinnacle I was thrumming with a fervent zeal. I stepped onto the landing and saw before me such a...'.

IT WAS HERE that the next few lines of script on the page became indecipherable, blotted out by some brackish fluid that had seeped into the paper. Where it became legible once more it continued:

'A RENAISSANCE of vestigial sensations permeated me as I peered deeper into the seemingly infinite geometry hidden therein. One could lose themselves there and think themselves fortunate for it. I ebbed and flowed, waxed and waned, stretched infinitely and contracted infinitesimally. Of all the words of all the exotic languages of man there wasn't a combination of such sufficient enough to lend justice to the events that unfolded there. I divided and multiplied and became each individual facet of myself laid bare before the scrupulous witness of all creation. And now I know that my weak and pallid flesh is but a prison destined for fester and rot. How can I possibly carry out the rest of my allotted days confined to these limited boundaries after having been scattered to the farthest reaches?'

THIS EXCERPT ENDED and flowed immediately into the next:

'ITS SCINTILLATING TONAL resonance calls upon me in my dreams, beseeching my return. Such longing cannot be contained within the finite boundaries of the human psyche and I ache to drift untethered within its fractal womb once more. I must return and commune again, if only for a little while. Sleep will never find me again unless I obey this summons.'

. . .

THE FOLLOWING pages were filled with incomprehensible scribbles, diagrams and sketches of repeating patterns in coalescing concentric circles growing steadily tighter and denser until the center was just a black hole bored through several pages with the ragged tip of a graphite pencil. Then, on the last page that contained text, amidst heavy, long dried droplets of what I could only imagine to be blood there was one final entry:

'I'VE NOT KNOWN such secrets in all my life. It wants to be revealed, to be heard, witnessed, its validity made manifest through recognition like some ancient exhibitionist. I am that witness, chosen to testify to its unquestionable authority. I am the vessel and I am the conduit. I shed these gristly folds of flesh, these damp and fetid bones, absolve myself of meat and matter until all that remains of me is teeth and tongue and lips and lungs to breathe life into these truths I've been entrusted to impregnate into the world!'

THE HOUR WAS both late and early by the time I had finished my reading. Despite the coffee I'd had earlier I was feeling drained and wanted sleep. It was a surprisingly daunting ordeal to relive this man's haunting account but I had a lead, a small unnamed seaside town somewhere relatively near Ellsworth. In the pale light of pre-dawn morning I rose from my chair and carried myself back to bed but this time my sleep was anything but dreamless.

I DREAMT OF A THICK DARKNESS, humid and warm, my skin slick with moisture. Taking rapid, hitching breaths I was assaulted by a heavy musty scent laced with sour rancid rot. I gagged in the blackness feeling the gorge rising in my parched throat. The ghastly miasma choked the atmosphere around my uncomfortably clammy naked flesh. Some coarse and damp leathery membrane enveloped me, pressing in from all sides, condensing my body into a fetal sphere. I struggled, straining against the malleable veil but failing to gain purchase as my hands and feet slipped futility across the mucousy secretions that coated my surroundings. As the terror rose with my gorge so did a great and unspeakable panic well up from some deep and long forgotten place of irrational childlike fear. I succumbed as the horror took me and I flailed recklessly against that terrible and unearthly womb until I felt the membrane weaken and I, with as much resolve as I could muster, pushed through. Just a hand at first, then an arm. Slowly I rend my way through until the membrane lost all integrity and I came spilling out onto a cold and smooth stone floor, viscous fluid pooling around me. Before I could gather my senses an incomprehensibly deep trumpet sounded sourcelessly. The sheer reverberation threatening to sunder me, to scatter the very atoms that hold me into a singular cohesive whole and reduce me to nothing more than cosmic matter. Curled in on myself, bare and vulnerable upon that stone, frantically clawing at my ears as my circulatory system ruptured and burst, that is when I woke.

PART II - TOMMY

When I returned to consciousness I did so rapidly, the late midday sun spilling across the bed through the open slatted blinds of my bedroom window. I was dreadfully hot and my white sheets clung to the sweat that covered my body. It was early afternoon when I dragged myself from bed, took a cold shower, and began packing for the trip to come. A single piece of luggage sufficed. After my clothes were neatly organized I tucked my loaded Colt M1917 revolver into its worn leather shoulder holster and placed it within the suitcase alongside two additional pre-loaded moon clips. I'd carried the Colt religiously during the war and it has always served me well. I wasn't expecting any trouble on this particular job but things have a way of happening precisely when you aren't expecting them to, and ever since I laid my eyes on that journal a quivering unease had taken root inside me. The revolver brought me comfort, the dense weight of its heavy case hardened steel frame giving the illusion of authority. Lastly, I added that damned journal to my effects before closing my suitcase.

. . .

WITH THE PREPARATION all but finished I hastily grabbed a few more simple necessities, picked up the keys to my Plymouth DeLuxe and was on the road north towards Ellsworth shortly before 4pm.

It was roughly a four hour commute to Ellsworth and so I decided to travel with haste if I was to spot this unnamed seaside town before nightfall. Yet, three hours and twenty minutes later the sun slipped beneath the horizon. Twilights otherworldly pall descended as the headlights of my Plymouth illuminated a harshly weathered wooden sign declaring 'Welcome to Ellsworth!'. I pulled onto the shoulder of the road and sat in the idling car for a moment considering whether to continue into Ellsworth for the evening and try once more in the morning or to turn around now and continue my search. After consulting both my map and the journal I felt confident that in my efforts to outpace the coming night I had grown careless and simply over-looked the turnoff. I decided that if I hadn't discovered what I was searching for within the next hour I would double back to find lodging in Ellsworth. I stowed the map on the seat beside me, lit a cigarette, and pulled off the shoulder into a U-turn.

I can't say for certain how long I drove before I found it but it must have been longer than the aforementioned hour I'd allotted myself. At some point I became so entranced by the barren road rushing through the yellow cone of my headlights and the soft lulling purr of the engine that I lost focus and my eyelids grew heavy. The wind whistled in the windows and the trees on either side of the road became a blur of greens and browns. I found myself drifting when the scent filled the automobile, bringing me back to my senses as my stomach contracted and I fought to stifle an immediate nausea. Every breath I drew was thick with putres-cence, brine and sewage.

· · ·

THERE WAS movement in my periphery and I snapped my head towards the passenger seat as my right hand instinctively moved under my overcoat for the revolver, the revolver that wasn't there. The revolver that was still in the goddamned...

MY HAND FROZE in place before I could finish that thought as my eyes fell upon the passenger seat. There sat the terrible visage of a small boy slumped forward, his head swinging limply with the swaying of the vehicle. Water fell in droplets from a tangled mess of black hair riddled with detritus and leaves. The boy was drenched, his frayed and rotting clothes plastered to his small frame. With a sharp snap the head lurched upright then fell backwards and came to rest against the right shoulder, as if the neck hadn't had any support whatsoever. I witnessed the boy's face for the first time and my eyes widened in horror as my mouth stuttered wordlessly. The flesh was bloated and ashen gray with slick green algae creeping along the left cheek into the hairline. One eye was a ruined and pulverized mass of congealing ichor. The other eye was clouded over with a thick milky cataract that peered aimlessly out from the puckered and swollen skin of his socket. The right side of his jaw was a ragged wound exposing a mandible draped in slack tendons and thick flaps of rubbery meat that dangled from the bone.

THE SPLIT BLUE lips parted and a mouthful of murky fluid cascaded over the chin as the boy spat out a single word with a wet exhalation of stagnant breath, "Eddy."

. . .

I STARED on in mute terror as the boy slowly raised an arm and dragged the back of one decomposing hand across his mouth as if to wipe the liquid away, but as he did so the tumefied, engorged lips simply sloughed off, revealing pale lacerated gums mottled with contusions and yellowed child teeth. The teeth parted and the boy reached into his mouth with the small fingers of his right hand and effortlessly raked the front teeth from the decayed gums of his lower jaw. My skin still crawls as I recall hearing them clatter to the floorboard. Removing his hand I could see clearly into his festering maw as his black distended tongue probed the dark viscous sludge that seeped from the now vacant and raw sockets in the mutilated gums. The tongue then traveled beyond, tentatively exploring the shredded tissue where the lips once were before the boy turned his attention back to me and wheezed, "where were you, Eddy? I waited so long."

IN MY SUDDEN inescapable panic I pressed myself against the driver's side door, entirely abandoning the wheel, desperately attempting to put as much space as possible between that thing and myself. I never saw the bend in the road, or the tree for that matter.

I came to consciousness hearing the soft patter of rain on the steel roof. There was a deep, aching throb in my brow above my right eye and the interior of the car was hazy with acrid white smoke. I cranked the window down, coughing and wafting the smoke away from my face. It cleared out easily enough and I promptly turned my attention to the passenger seat once more looking for any sign of the child and finding none. No boy, no teeth on the floorboard. Just the map where I'd placed it, and yet the fabric of the seat was undeniably and inexplicably wet to the touch.

. . .

THE PASSENGER SIDE window had apparently shattered from the impact though. I looked at my wrist watch, which had fortunately survived the accident. The hands read a quarter to one. If I'd been unconscious for that long it was plausible that the rain may be responsible for the damp fabric of the seat but with no way of knowing how long it had been raining that train of thought was little more than conjecture. My head was swimming. I struck a match from the glovebox and took a deep drag off of a cigarette as I sat there for a few minutes collecting myself and recounting that gut wrenching nightmare. There wasn't an iota of doubt in my mind. That was little Tommy Hershel.

PART III - THE SUMMER OF 1908

When I was a boy myself, no more than twelve years old, I had a friend by the name of Emmett Hershel who lived four houses down the street from me. Last I'd heard good old Emmett perished valiantly during the battle of Belleau Wood but long before the war he and I would ride our bicycles through the forest outside of town. We'd built many a fort, tree house and dam in those woods, caught all manner of creature and critter alike.

Well, Emmett had a little brother named Tommy who would often tag along with us. Tommy was only a few years younger than Emmett but when you're twelve a few years feels like more than it is and we often jibed Tommy for being the runt. One day in the early summer of 1908 while the three of us pioneered our way deeper into the woods we stumbled across a small creek and followed it upstream flipping rocks and looking for crawfish as we went. After an hour or so we'd traced the creek to the mouth of an old stone storm drain tunnel covered in a heavy rusted steel grate barring the entrance. It seems like such a small thing now but at the time it was a discovery of monumental proportions.

. . .

TRY as we may we couldn't prize the heavy metallic gate free, despite there being no apparent lock in place.

WE WERE all but ready to surrender to the impenetrable stone tunnel when Tommy spied a glimmer of some minuscule refractive object that caught the late afternoon sunlight beyond the grate amidst the accrued debris within the tunnel. We three pressed our faces between the filthy bars, cupping our hands around our eyes as best we could to take the edge off of the glare, squinting to make out just what that shimmer might have been. It was I that finally realized what that irresistibly tantalizing glean was originating from: a single large cat's eye marble of deep emerald glass. A shooter, that's what we called them back then. Emmett and I noted it with passive interest, accepting that the marble was out of reach. Tommy, on the other hand, grew enamored with the marble, as kids were oft to do when it came to small bobbles and the sort.

THE LONG TREK back through the forest was rife with chatter from little Tommy, easily a thousand different ideas on how to gain access to the tunnel, on odd and fantastical contraptions to retrieve the marble. None of them sounded very plausible but Emmett and I, with a sidelong glance at one another, reached an unspoken agreement that neither of us would say as much. I soon forgot about the marble all together as but only four days later Tommy Hershel went unexpectedly missing.

. . .

NEEDLESS TO SAY, my boyhood friendship with Emmett fell into decline after that. I never held it against him and one could hardly fault him for growing distant. The Hershel family had a difficult time ahead of them but three months later their lives were beginning to return to a semblance of normality. During that time I'd resumed my occasional exploratory expeditions in the nearby forests, albeit by that time I was traveling alone. I couldn't say at the time just what urged me to wander back to that old storm drain tunnel but on one particular afternoon I decided to return to the stream and trace it back to the mouth of that impenetrable tunnel. It was early evening when I finally arrived and the sun was nearing the horizon. I remember it being miserably hot. I was winded from the hike and soaked in my own perspiration. Sitting upon one of the large rocks that littered the clearing to catch my breath I thought about the thrashing I was in for when I returned home. Back then I had a strict curfew. I was to be home by dusk and my father wasn't afraid of enforcing it. He was a good man, mind you, and a good father as well but he had a firm hand and applied it liberally when necessary.

The cicadas droned restlessly nearby as a cool breeze stirred in the treetops and I was grateful for it, that is until the scent it carried struck me, the very same sickening smell that assailed me in my automobile. Stale, stagnant water and pungent fetid decay. The creeping of goose flesh crawled its way up the nape of my neck as I stood. I slowly and cautiously ambled toward the grated mouth of the tunnel. As I approached and peered between the bars I noticed a shaft of dim light piercing the darkness diagonally from above. It appeared that some of the old stonework had crumbled and caved inward revealing a small hole in the top of the tunnel. As my eyes followed the shaft of light downward my breath caught in my throat.

. . .

THERE WAS LITTLE TOMMY, partially submerged and softly undulating on the surface of the glassy black water. The small body was so distended with bloat that he was hardly recognizable. He floated on his back, white cloudy eyes staring blankly, or perhaps longingly, upward towards the hole he no doubt climbed in through only to discover he couldn't climb out again. His lips had been gnawed away by rats rendering what remained of the mouth a nightmarish grinning rictus of pale gray gums and bared teeth. The black hair of his head had begun to fall away in large clots, his scalp softened by the constant exposure to the water, and what remained drifted lazily around his gently bobbing head. It seemed that Tommy had not forgotten about the marble.

The smell that emanated from within is a smell I've carried with me my entire life, and whether it be an animal carcass rotting alongside the road or the moldering corpses of soldiers fallen and left behind, whenever I catch the scent of decay it's always Tommy that I'm smelling.

Now, I've had nightmares before, vivid and terrible recollections of the war where I'd find myself on the frontlines and in the trenches once again. Nightmares so engrossing and so gripping that when I'd wake I'd find myself upon the floor or even in another room. I'd not dreamt of Tommy in twenty years and never had I ever experienced a dream that felt so palpably visceral.

<h1 style="text-align:center">PART IV - PORT CAIRN</h1>

I spent several long minutes in the driver's seat revisiting the vestigial remnants of my childhood trauma. Once my nerves had settled I opened the car door and stumbled out, scolding myself for falling asleep at the wheel. It was a mistake easily avoided had I only stopped for the night in Ellsworth. The rain had staunched itself to little more than a misty drizzle. I flicked the smoldering stub of my lucky and began inspecting the damage to the Plymouth. Thick white smoke billowed up from the steel chassis. A decidedly resilient tree was girdled by the front axle and had become as much a part of the automobile as the engine itself. Although one headlight was still functional it was clear that my vehicle wasn't going anywhere any time soon. I was left with no choice but to find this mysterious town lest I became stranded there. The prospect of being marooned along that barren stretch of road did not sit well with me. It was oppressively dark and the night had grown uncomfortably chill despite the wool overcoat I wore.

. . .

I WENT to the trunk and retrieved my revolver, removing my coat and taking a moment to affix the supple leather holster underneath my left arm. I then slipped the additional moon clips into my outer left pocket. That being done I gathered both map and journal before returning to the road.

Stepping back onto the earthen byway I deduced that to my right was the direction from which I'd approached and as such that way would eventually lead back to Ellsworth but traveling that distance on foot was not much of an option. There was enough moonlight breaking through the gossamer cloud cover to make out the monochromatic surroundings until they either became obscured by low mists or vanished into the dense shadows of the forest. Knowing that I couldn't be far from my intended destination I continued down the road on foot.

THE NIGHT WAS EERILY static and the stillness there instilled a sense of permanence and isolation, as if this lonesome stretch of road existed elsewhere, detached from time and space and wholly separated from the comforting familiarity of earth and by extension I was as well. As I walked the only sound to be heard was that of my footfalls atop the gravelly surface of that road. Paranoia and what was admittedly fear soon took a firm grasp on my faculties. The shadows around me took on a life of their own, shifting and skulking in my periphery only to cease their ambling perambulations the moment I fixed my gaze upon them. Each time I'd turn back to the road ahead I'd be taken by a growing certainty that some unseen stalking menace was creeping ever closer and it was solely my gaze keeping it at bay.

.   .   .

I KNEW this to be merely a fantastical manifestation of course, the product of an overactive imagination, but in moments such as those logic is easily stifled by the overbearing conviction of fear. Instinct urged me to quicken my pace and I soon found myself moving at a brisk trot. I forced myself to stop, reminding myself that I was being unreasonable, and that is when I noticed it.

Roughly ten feet from where I stood there was an easily over-looked break in the foliage that marked the partition between forest and road. Harshly overgrown and under-traveled the only distinguishing feature that suggested it was a road of sorts was the absence of trees. Having seen no other tangential offshoots from the main road I knew I had at long last discovered the path that would lead me to my destination. I was so overcome with renewed vigor at this minor victory that all the lurking phantasms and specters that previously vexed me dissolved into vapor. I steeled my resolve and, leaving the road behind, took my first steps down the dark and densely wooded path.

The ground was largely obfuscated by a heavy fog and traversing the overgrown foliage became recklessly precarious. That, in conjunction with the oppressive darkness, made navigating this path nearly impossible. The only source of light on my person was that of my tarnished kerosene lighter. Fishing it from out my inner breast pocket I struck the wheel and was momentarily blinded by the incendiary flash. Allowing my eyes to adjust for a moment it became obvious to me just how densely concentrated the forest was. So short was the breadth of the path that the sinister silhouettes of the trees seemed to press in from either side. Nonetheless, I had light, although how long it would last was dubious at best.

. . .

FROM THERE IT was a fairly straightforward path and within the hour I saw distant lights through the trees that had steadily grown thinner as I drew nearer to the coast. The air was laced with brine and saltwater and if I listened closely the far off sound of crashing waves could be heard. I saw that I was approaching from a position of slight elevation as the path wound down to the town proper. It was there that I had my first true sight of the sea and the small town nestled along its shore. I could see in stark contrast to the pallid moonlight dancing across the surface of the ocean waters the silhouettes of half a dozen ships anchored at the docks of the harbor, bobbing indolently. I also noticed the most prominent landmark in view, the tall spire of a lighthouse perched upon an outcropping of rock a ways from shore.

SEEING the town laid out before me I suddenly felt very fatigued, the daunting ordeals of the last 24 hours seeming to catch up to me all at once. Glancing down at my wristwatch I saw that the hour had grown very late, approaching 3 o'clock in the morning. With what little fortitude I had left within me I pressed onward into town. I passed an intricately carved wooden sign that simply read "Port Cairn", the sharp edges worn smooth from countless years of being buffeted by the seaside air. When I first entered the town I thought it vacant.

The emptiness of those streets was unlike anything I'd seen in Boston. Even at an hour such as this there would have been vagrants and derelicts wandering about. Here there wasn't so much as the errant stray dog in sight. All was silent save for the crashing of waves, whose audibility was amplified by the stillness which saturated the atmosphere.

. . .

THE STREET I was walking along was of cobbled stone and I could see that the smattering of lights I'd glimpsed earlier were quaint lampposts placed periodically along either side of the road. There were a number of structures and domiciles within sight, each with its own darkened windows as well as a number of various establishments that sat nestled in the shadows between the lampposts.

The only thing I was concerned about at that moment though was locating lodging for the evening. Striding deeper into the uncharted town of Port Cairn I was vigilant for any such venue that may offer a room for the remainder of the night. After turning left at a central intersection I did indeed happen upon a homely alehouse that advertised available accommodations. The establishment didn't present the most attractive facade but it was open for business at this hour and that was, arguably, the only point of interest that mattered. The title above the entryway read "Tensman and Tenant" and as I stepped within the dimly illuminated interior I was met with the residual scent of stale beer and woodsmoke. I stood in an brief foyer.

TO THE IMMEDIATE left was a wide set of closed heavy wooden doors, a ways beyond that at the end of this foyer was a staircase and to my right a short reception counter. Seated behind this counter was a bespectacled man in his later years that must have been hard of hearing as he didn't take notice of my arrival until I stepped into the light of the desk lamp at his side and announced my presence. He introduced himself as Clyde Tensman but beyond that our interaction was brief, he was a man of few words and I was a man on the cusp of collapsing where I stood.

. . .

I PROMPTLY PAID the gentleman $2.50 for a room, watched as he turned and pulled a slender brass key from a hook on the wall behind him and bid him a good evening as I walked up the stairs, making my way to the room. Once inside I kicked my shoes from my feet, allowed my coat to fall to the hardwood floor and sank into the welcoming and surprisingly comfortable mattress.

UNCONSCIOUSNESS MUST HAVE WASHED over me within moments. I drifted serenely, suspended without tether in the boundless void of ignorant bliss. Very suddenly I found myself curled into a fetal position, slick with viscous prenatal fluids, shivering and nude against the frigid unyielding stone ground beneath me. Slowly I pulled myself to my knees, and then my feet. My vision panned the surroundings and I witnessed thousands of large leathery chrysalises suspended vertically in space gently rotating silently a few feet above the ground. I turned back to see the one I had wrested free from performing it's own soundless pirouette, occasionally spilling a mass of wet membranous tissue to the stone below. These terrible cocoons spanned as far as the eye could see. My frenetic heart was pounding within my heaving chest as I breathed rapidly. Panic threatened to overtake me as I broke into a mad sprint, serpentining through the blackly iridescent chitinous chrysalises. I had no direction, no landmarks or means of navigating that endlessly repeating hive of slumbering horrors and the clandestine chimeras that lie dormant there. After fleeing aimlessly for what felt like an eternity I stumbled and spilled onto my hands and knees. I remained there, my lungs searing with every gulping breath. I tentatively raised my head fearing that I'd be met with the same hopelessly infinite expanse of pupating stasis. Instead, before me at a distance impossible to deduce across a vast and barren plane of ochre stone, rose a monolithic jagged obsidian spire of towering heights so utterly brobdingnagian in scale as to render the totality of my minuscule and myopic existence wholly insignificant by relation. Atop the unseen pinnacle of this spire there emanated an eldritch purpureal radiance that washed over the entirety of the foreboding landscape in pulsing waves, persistent and deliberate in consistent intervals. With each passing pulse I felt the light physically seeping into my skin, my flesh and bones soaking it in and gluttonously drinking it up. I was awash with ancient and primordial power thrumming within every taut fiber of my fragile being. I let loose an involuntary scream of both anguish and ecstasy as the pressure building inside my feeble organic structure threatened to split me open and crawl it's way through, shedding my worthless flesh to emerge reborn and renewed and I ached for it longingly. I was struck in that moment with a revelation of indescribable magnitude. It was as though a beacon had illuminated every inscrutable mystery that life has held selfishly out of reach and I had the answer to the question every man that has ever lumbered the earth has asked themselves in vain futility; "What is my purpose?".

In that moment I knew precisely what my purpose was. I threw my head back and bellowed into eternity:

"I AM THE COCOON! I AM THE CHRYSALIS!"

I SLEPT LATE the next morning, not stirring until 10am. When I did wake I found that I was voraciously famished. The man I spoke to the previous night had offered me a $.50 up charge for breakfast which I foolishly declined in my near delusional fatigue. Taking in the room around me in the daylight it wasn't quite as agreeable as I'd found it the night before. The bed was comfortable enough and the room fulfilled its function but if I was to remain in Port Cairn for several days I preferred finer lodging. It then occurred to me that perhaps I could kill two birds with a single stone.

I fetched the repugnant journal from my coat upon the floor and began scouring the stained pages for any mention of where the author may have stayed while in town. In a short time I did indeed find a brief entry not long after his arrival in town that mentioned a "charming seaside inn just off the harbor with a picturesque view of the coast. Meridians End is an exceptional venue to enjoy a day or two of leisure and I may have unwittingly stumbled into a potential sale with the Innkeeper, Meredith Shoals. Only time will tell."

With a heading I gathered my scant belongings and made my way outside, stopping briefly to return the room key on my way out. Emerging from the interior of the alehouse I was greeted by a dismally dreary overcast sky, typical for that time of year in the northeast. The town of Port Cairn wasn't all that much more welcoming in the light of day than in the dead of night. An air of begrudging concession laid heavy over the townsfolk who themselves projected a collective atmosphere of defeat. The day was chill and there was a sharp, biting breeze, a portent of the coming approach of winter. I buttoned the front of my coat and bent my head against the winds blowing in off the ocean and made my way towards the harbor. It wasn't difficult to find due to the simple construction of the town.

Port Cairn was a town built around a central crossroads, the main street running directly through town and terminating at the docks. Branching from the crossroads were several snaking byways leading to outlying structures that seemed to me not unlike sheep that had strayed from the flock. The town was most dense near the crossroads and slowly began to lose cohesion the farther one drifted from its center, with the sole exception being the wharf. The raucous screech of seagulls heralded my arrival. I paused and inhaled deeply, savoring the salinity of the sea and admiring the unparalleled majesty of the tumultuous ocean.

Watching those foamy white-capped waves churn beneath the blackened sky brought to mind that captivating painting by Mr. Hammond, "The Maelstrom". All but two ships were absent from harbor, not unusual for midday. I glanced around for anyone that might perchance point me in the direction of Meridian's End. There was a man seated at the end of the pier casting a fishing pole into the shallows, two children sitting on the stoop of what appeared to be a bakery, from which emanated a most desirable aroma, and another man alongside one of the ships, a fishing vessel, in the process of tying the mooring. I thought it best to address the latter as currently he was in closest proximity and seemed to carry himself with a degree of familiarity.

As I approached him I announced my presence so as to not startle the man.

"Excuse me." I said a little louder than necessary to ensure he heard me.

The gentleman looked backwards over his shoulder in my direction and I raised my hand in a brief wave.

"Pardon my intrusion, I hope I'm not interrupting. I was wondering if you might assist me?"

He straightened his posture from the bent position over the mooring with a minor groan and replied, "all depends on what ya need but I'll see what I can do for ya."

The man was grizzled to say the least. He'd spent more days at sea than not by the looks of his unkempt ivory beard and weathered skin. He couldn't have been less than 50 years old but still appeared quite capable. I extended my right hand and he accepted it in a calloused, firm handshake.

. . .

"I APPRECIATE YOUR TIME. I'm new to town and I'm afraid I'm not familiar with the area just yet. I could use some direction. Could you show me the way to Meridian's End?"

THE MAN PEERED at me curiously before replying, "Sure, I can help ya with that. I didn't catch your name, stranger. It's not often that we draw outsiders here."

"FORGIVE ME, my name is Edmond. I likely won't be in town for long. I'm passing through on some business and heard that Meridian's End was a fine place to stay for a night or two."

"YES SIR, that it is. It's a few hundred yards down thataway." Here he raised an arm and pointed down the left hand side of the dock. "Last building before the open shoreline. Can't miss it. It's got a great big porch with a railing that runs round it pieced together from driftwood. When you get there tell Meredith that Cliff sent ya. She'll take good care of ya."

"AWFULLY KIND OF YOU, Cliff. Thank you once more for the aid." With that we parted ways.

I WISHED to arrive at Meridian's End in a timely fashion but I was dreadfully hungry and so I decided to purchase a few fresh pastries from the bakery to eat as I walked. Embarking in the direction given, it wasn't long before I found myself alone along the boardwalk as there weren't many wayfarers or commerce to be had that far from the central harbor. The structures to my left slid gradually into progressive states of disrepair the farther I travelled until many of them were simply abandoned and surrendered to the elements. To my right remained the restless ocean dashing itself against the rocks that acted as a breakwater and there in the distance, standing vigil over all of Port Cairn, was the towering lighthouse seeming to rise from out the ocean depths.

EVENTUALLY I REACHED the end of the established path before there was only the sandy, windswept coastline ahead of me and there, as promised, was one final building standing apart and alone. It was an endearing establishment that resembled a three story cottage more than an inn. There was a large picketed perimeter enclosing an ample interior with tall tufts of beach grass rustling in the winds. Within the outer fence stood Meridian's End, although there was no sign or lettering declaring it as such. I entered through the fence and strode down the walkway, up a few steps and onto a broad porch whose outer railing was indeed tastefully constructed from an impressive array of drift-wood. A small hand painted sign hung within the glass panes of the front door which read "Open". I entered, tolling a small bell over the doorway and was immediately met with the spicy aroma of freshly baked apple pie.

.   .   .

Within I found welcome respite from the cutting seaside winds and I inhaled deeply, savoring the warmth as it flooded my person. The interior was indeed much like that of a large cottage and seemed intentionally so. I stood within the doorway looking about for where I might check in but it became apparent that Meridian's End was not that sort of inn and so I patiently waited, trusting that the chiming of the bell would be answered shortly. There was a clamorous metallic clang from somewhere farther within and an exasperated sigh followed by an upbeat if not somewhat overwhelmed female voice that said loudly "Be with you in just a moment".

A minute or so passed before a woman appeared from the far end of a corridor that ran adjacent to where I was currently standing. She was a slight woman of slender build and the subtle luster of occasional gray hidden among her dark auburn hair in conjunction with the noticeable creasing at the corners of her eyes suggested that she was in her early to mid forties. The state of her hair was somewhat frazzled and there was a light perspiration upon her brow. She wore a genuine and warm smile that extended to her eyes, eyes that I could then see displayed a distinct and dull pearlescent film. They never seemed to fix on any specific focal point but rather stared vacantly off into the distance and it was then that it occurred to me this woman was mostly, if not entirely blind.

As she met me where I stood she said, "Hello and welcome! I'm terribly sorry to have made you wait. I like to prepare a home cooked supper for the guests. I find that it provides a personal touch not easily found elsewhere."

. . .

IN CLOSE PROXIMITY I perceived that she looked dreadfully tired and yet her movements and mannerisms were manic. She spoke rapidly and with an almost enraptured enthusiasm.

"No need to apologize whatsoever, ma'am. Please, pardon my untimely intrusion. Allow me to introduce myself, my name is Edmond. Might you perhaps be Mrs. Shoals?"

HAVING ANNOUNCED my location those vacuous eyes shifted and fell upon my face for the first time and the smile with which she'd greeted me dropped quite unexpectedly. There was such a sudden shift in the dynamic of her demeanor that I was taken aback. A torrent of conflicting micro expressions flashed across her face in rapid succession before, just as quickly, she found her smile once more, only now it didn't quite reach her eyes.

"Your arrival is no intrusion at all," she replied. The tone of her voice now noticeably less upbeat. "I am indeed Mrs. Shoals. I take it that you'd like to rent a room?"

I HAD YET to understand just what had transpired but a moment ago and I answered hesitantly, "...Yes. Yes, that is correct. If there are any vacancies, that is."

Not only had her demeanor shifted but her body language had as well. It was as if she had shrunk in on herself, somehow become smaller, meeker. She'd developed an observable tremor in her left hand and was attempting to conceal it beneath the apron she was wearing.

"Oh yes. They're all vacant. Not many tourists out this way, I fear. You may take your pick among any of the rooms and I'm certain you'll be pleased with all of them. How long will you be staying?"

. . .

"It's difficult to say but I'd venture roughly a week or so. I'd be happy to pay in advance, of course."

With a sharp bark of forced laughter she said, "Nonsense, you may pay as you go. I don't expect this old place will fill up anytime soon. Now let me show you our rooms."

"Well, about that. I have an odd request if you'd find it permissible. There was a gentleman with whom I was acquainted that had stayed here a number of years ago. A traveling salesman if I recall correctly. His name has since slipped my mind but I was hoping that you may remember him? I understand that isn't the most informative description but unfortunately it's all I've got to go off of."

Her cloudy eyes drifted away from my face and her gaze grew distant once more. She remained expressionless and eerily absent for perhaps a little longer than I was comfortable with before her right brow twitched abruptly and the entirety of her demeanor's polarity switched yet again. She seemed to be lost in thought before replying through a coquettish grin that easily made her appear 15 years younger.

"Oh, it has been many a year since I last revisited those memories. I remember him well. I was quite smitten with him if you don't mind my saying so. Handsome as the devil and a sterling tongue to boot. His name was Maynard, I believe. Why do you ask?" she queried as she cocked her head to the side inquisitively. She was almost childlike at that moment.

. . .

I WAS ALARMINGLY CONFUSED and beginning to think it likely that she was a bit unstable.

"Well, it was this very gentleman's description of his time spent here that prompted my own stay and I should say that I'd be most agreeable to occupying the same chambers as he once did. Can you be certain this is the same man?"

WITH LITTLE HESITATION Mrs. Shoals responded, "Quite certain, I'm sure. To my knowledge there hasn't been a traveling salesman passing through these parts before or since. As you can see, Port Cairn isn't the most accessible town and Meridians End lies on the outskirts of that so visitors are few and far between. As for that room in particular, allow me to retrieve the key for you."

"Of course. Thank you kindly." I said, not bothering to inquire as to how she remembered which room this man stayed in. I was fairly certain I knew and I had no desire to embarrass her.

WITH THAT SHE walked through a doorway on the right and soon returned holding a tarnished key ring. "If you'll follow me, I will lead you to your room."

Trailing behind, I followed her through an archway and down a narrow corridor. How she managed to navigate without the aid of sight was beyond me. She stopped before a dark wooden door that had a brass placard displaying the number 3 tacked to the front of it. She shuffled through the keys and placed one within the keyhole before turning it with a soft metallic click. The door swung inward revealing a comfortable and homely room within. She took a moment to remove the key from the key ring and held it before her, waiting for me to accept it.

· · ·

I PEERED down at the small key resting in her upturned palm and then at her face and hazy distant eyes. I began extending my arm to retrieve the key when the faintly varicosed flesh around her left eye constricted tightly, giving the impression that she was squinting with that eye. Without warning the muscles on the left side of her face went slack. The skin there lost all cohesion and hung loosely, It's structural integrity abandoned.

Mrs. Shoals appeared none too perturbed by this alarming occurrence as she continued calmly standing before me, arm extended. One corner of her mouth was sagging dramatically while the other continued to broadly smile. Her left eye, mostly obscured by the drooping lid and nestled amidst the folds, was hardly visible. Her visage was ambiguously grotesque and deeply unsettling, like some grisly amalgamation of the ancient and dipolar thespian masks, simultaneously both comedic and tragic.

With a violent twinge the flaccid corner of her mouth involuntarily twitched and fluttered spasmodically, and then, slowly, the muscles of her face contracted once more. Still she stood before me holding the key and waiting. I swiftly withdrew my hand and took a step backwards.

"Is something the matter, Edmond?", she asked kindly.

I couldn't quite place just what it was, but some facet of what had just taken place stirred within me a great and lingering unease. I was assuredly concerned for the wellbeing of Mrs. Shoals and thought it possible that I'd perhaps just witnessed a stroke, but she didn't miss a beat. There was no trace of acknowledgment. No variance in behavior before, during, or after the incident.

SWIFTLY COMPOSING MYSELF, I replied in a voice more shaken than I'd anticipated, "On the contrary, Meredith, are you well? I fear you've just suffered a fit of some kind."

She laughed sheepishly, "Meredith? How forward of you, Edmond. A fit, you say? I don't feel as though I've just suffered a fit. I feel quite fine, in fact." She said dismissively. With a few short steps she closed the distance between us, placed the key in my hand and pressed her palm against my back as she guided me into the room. "Now, enjoy your stay. I hope the accommodations are to your liking and if you need anything at all please don't hesitate to ask."

Once within the doorway of the room I turned to face her and said "Of, coarse. I appreciate your hospitality and thank you for obliging my admittedly outlandish requests."

"It's no bother at all. Get yourself situated. Dinner is at 6:30. I look forward to seeing you then."

AS SHE TURNED AWAY and began to depart a thought occurred to me and I called after her, "Oh, Mrs. Shoals, a few minutes ago you'd mentioned that you like to prepare dinner for the guests, but then you said that there aren't any occupants at the moment. If that's the case then who are you preparing dinner for?"

Without turning back she spoke over her shoulder, "For you, of course. Welcome to Meridians End, Mr. Jameson." She then disappeared around the corner and out of sight.

I HAD NOT GIVEN her my surname.

.   .   .

AFTER MRS. SHOALS took her leave I familiarized myself with my room. There was a generously sized bed butted against the wall to the right flanked by a pair of bedside tables, each of which bearing its own small lamp with shades of stained glass. There was a modest writing desk against the far wall that sat before a window with a picturesque view of the sea and the towering, cyclopean lighthouse. On the left side of the room was a rustic dresser beside a slender doorway that led into a meager but functional lavatory that contained both toilet and sink. Along the walls there hung a variety of paintings portraying thalassic themes and marine scenery. The entirety of Meridians End was tastefully shy of being obscenely saccharine and it would seem that Meredith had a calculating eye for decor and atmosphere.

The floorboards beneath my feet groaned in protest as I strode across the room to the desk and removed my coat, which I draped over the simple chair that was placed there. I haphazardly tossed the journal upon the desktop and breathed a heavy sigh of relief. It was as if the knowledge of having the journal upon my person had been steadily chafing my subconscious mind, not prominent enough to be immediately recognizable but subtle and persistent enough to swell unnoticed into an all-permeant malaise that had unknowingly saturated my well-being, only revealed through its sudden absence.

I stood there, looking down upon that repugnant journal and considered the possibility that this was not the first time it had sat upon this particular desk. His name was Maynard. I have always felt a sense of ghostly disquiet when standing in the exact spot that those I'm investigating have once stood, taking in the same environment that they once did. There is an uncanny feeling of replicated experience, that I am either an extension of their perception or that this shared perspective has been recycled and reconstituted by some incomparable celestial machine.

. . .

IT WAS a sensation that made my spine quiver and yet I felt somehow intimately closer to Maynard for having experienced it.

A few hours passed and in that time I took inventory of just what I had at my disposal. There was my revolver and spare ammo, a pencil and my notebook, my wristwatch, a quarter pack of cigarettes, my lighter, roughly $200 and change within my wallet alongside my Private Investigators license, and lastly a small slip joint pocket knife. It didn't amount to much but an individual, if clever enough, could accomplish a great deal with very little.

Money can go a long way in acquiring goods and services and, in my experience, where money fails a gun prevails, if the end justifies the means. Placing my Colt revolver upon the desktop I dedicated several minutes to inspecting it and ensuring its functionality. I then secured it back into its harness and checked the time. It was nearing 6:30pm and Mrs. Shoals would be expecting me for dinner. That's not to say I wasn't excited by the prospect of a hot meal. The pastries I'd had earlier that day were hardly satiating and only served to take the edge off the mounting hunger. The last time I had truly eaten was the lunch I'd ended up violently expelling after returning from my meeting with Mr. Hammond and that was over 24 hours prior.

Needless to say, I was ravenous. No, truth be told I was more concerned with sharing another disturbing interaction with Meredith. The woman clearly wasn't well and I still hadn't processed just what in the hell had happened to her earlier. Nonetheless, she was kind enough to go through the trouble of cooking for me and I was more than happy to eat it. I slid the chair out and stood, stopping to admire the view beyond the window. The pale lighthouse stood out in stark contrast against a backdrop of dense sable thunderheads, even in the waning twilight.

. . .

A FLASH of radiance illuminated the roiling clouds from within and a low reverberant thunder rolled into shore. I found myself entranced with the distant storm and the picture it painted before me, whipping the waves into a frenzy before slamming themselves mercilessly against the sands. It seemed as if the slumbering sea had been roused by the crashing of thunder and was furiously attempting to crawl its way ashore.

I bent over, switched off the desk lamp and turned away from the desk just as a bolt of incandescent lightning set the room aglow with a flash. In that moment, as I was partway turned about, I thought I caught sight of something queer in the periphery of my vision. Something along the windowsill.

I switched the lamp on once more and leaned over the desk, running my fingers across the wood beneath the window. The light of the desk lamp was too flat, too direct, but the lightning cast a sharp light at just the precise angle to reveal something that had been faintly scribed into the wood and later painted over. I could feel the indentation beneath my fingertips but still could not make out just what had been carved there. If Maynard had indeed sat at that very desk and shared the same view then there was a solid probability that whatever was written there was left by none other than Maynard himself.

Quickly I rifled through my pockets and produced my notebook and pencil. Tearing a fresh sheet of paper from the notebook I laid it atop the windowsill and began feverishly rubbing the flat of the pencil's graphite tip across the page. When I was satisfied I turned the paper towards myself and there, in hastily hewn and harshly angular lines was a singular sentence that read

"To behold the Beacon is to be held by it." A curious, if not poignant statement no doubt referencing the lighthouse.

. . .

I FUMBLED FOR THE JOURNAL, flipping it over so that the cover was
exposed. I placed the sheet of paper beside it and thoroughly
compared the graphite rubbing to the sigil scrawled upon the
leather face of the journal. There was no mistake. The idio-
syncratic angles of the lines, the variances in pressure applied
with each stroke, the uncharacteristic tendency for the lines to
bisect one another, all these suggested that both the inscription
and the journal had been penned by the same hand.

An excitement welled up within me. If this cryptic message
had been left behind then surely there must have been more. As I
was preparing to perform a further investigation of the room I
heard Meredith's voice call out "Edmond. Are you joining me for
dinner?" I stopped mid step and looked down at my watch. It was
6:47. I had become so engrossed with the recent discoveries that I'd
completely lost track of time. I called back "Oh, yes! My apologies,
I'm afraid I dozed off. I'll be with you in just a moment."

I hurriedly made myself presentable and exited the room. A
savory aroma suffused the inn and as I made my way in the direction of the dining room I wasn't surprised to find myself exces-
sively salivating. I had my apprehensions regarding Meredith but
found those to be swiftly belayed by my voracious appetite, which
seemed in that moment to have more sway over my faculties than
logic did. Upon entering the dining room I saw laid out before me
such a banquet of decadence that one could scarcely consider it to
be anything so inadequate as dinner. I looked upon the ostentatious spread in veritable disbelief. There were dishes, platters,
bowls, boats, baskets, trays, and cloches that covered nearly every
inch of the tabletop. It was sheer hysteria. Standing on the far side
of the table was Meredith wearing a manic grin plastered across
her sweaty, flour dappled face.

. . .

HER HAIR WAS a frazzled disaster haphazardly pinned back and she looked upon the brink of exhaustion. This was hours worth of labor. I was speechless as I stood dumbfounded in the doorway staring slack jawed at the sumptuous feast before me.

"Well, don't just stand there. Come and have a seat. I'll fix you a plate." Her voice was soft and intimate in a way that caught me unawares.

I stammered inadvertently as I said "Mrs. Shoals, this is far too lavish. You must have worked yourself ragged to prepare all this! I couldn't possibly eat a third of all the food here."

She methodically began to sidle around the table, stopping at a chair and drawing it outward. "Nonsense, Edmond. It was no hassle whatsoever. We take care of our guests here at Meridians End." She gestured towards the chair and said, "won't you?"

Not wanting to appear unappreciative I slowly took the seat presented to me. I watched on in silence as Meredith produced a plate and set to filling it with a sampling of just about every dish upon the table before placing it down in front of me. Whatever suspicions I might have been harboring immediately dissolved as I laid eyes on the impressive mound of food.

Staring longingly at the plate in anticipation I absentmindedly said "Mrs. Shoals, this all looks so incredible. I can't remember the last time I've had a home cooked meal. I deeply appreciate you taking the time to cook all this."

I picked up the utensils and took a hearty bite of mashed potatoes as I tore my gaze away from the plate and realized that Meredith was no longer standing behind me. In fact, Meredith was no longer in the dining room at all and had slipped away without my noticing.

. . .

I THOUGHT it odd but was more invested in satiating my hunger so I continued eating under the assumption that she'd return shortly. As I ate I contemplated that obscure statement etched into the windowsill. I wondered just how long Maynard had stayed in Port Cairn. According to the journal he'd only intended to stay for an evening although I suspect his stay was far longer. My mind wandered down curious and speculative paths at what mysterious remnants may yet lie hidden within my room. It was very likely that I was chasing vapor, that there wasn't anything more to be revealed and I was simply hoping there would.

In either case the only way I'd know for certain was to give the room a thorough pass. I allowed my thoughts to drift unabated, the current of my curiosity carrying them where it may and before I knew it I'd finished every last scrap of food from off the plate before me. Time can be elusive that way. I leaned back in the chair, my stomach pleasantly full, and wondered what became of Meredith. She hadn't returned. I thought that perhaps she'd turned in early for the evening, not surprising considering just how depleted she seemed to be since my arrival. The table was laden with an excess of food and I couldn't in good conscience leave it out to spoil after all the effort Meredith had put into cooking it. With a heavy sigh I stood and began putting the food away. When that was finished I washed my plate in the sink, sat it aside and made my way back to my room.

Dinner had left me feeling sluggish but as I entered the room that familiar excitement once again took hold and my focus narrowed. I lit every lamp in the room, and considered where to start. Outside the wind was howling and I could hear the heavy rains pelting the roof above. It may seem like a cliche but asking yourself "Where would I" is surprisingly effective when searching for hidden effects.

· · ·

SYSTEMATICALLY I BEGAN at the left wall and made my way around the room, gently removing paintings as I went looking for any indication that the wallpaper had been tampered with. I then double checked by softly rapping my knuckles against the walls every few feet, listening for any variation in solidity. Satisfied that there was nothing hidden within the walls or beneath the wallpaper I investigated any lip or protrusion like that of the windowsill. I peered beneath the desk, on the underside of the chair, within the drawers and underneath the lamps for any further inscriptions. Still I found nothing. I felt along the inside of the mattress, scoured the bathroom and pulled the dresser away from the wall. Not a single thing.

I will admit I was growing increasingly disheartened. Surely there was something I was overlooking. From outside there sounded a resounding crash of deafening thunder that shook the glass of the window panes. I slowed my thoughts with a few deep breaths and performed a meticulous visual sweep of the room from the perspective of the bathroom doorway. I then laid eyes on that which I'd been missing. Concealed a few feet beneath the foot of the bed there was a blackened rectangular wrought iron grate flush with the hardwood floor. Some sort of ventilation duct most likely. I strode across the room and gently shoved the bed aside until there was enough clearance to access the duct unimpeded. Lowering myself onto my knees I dug the small slip joint knife from the recesses of my pocket.

I thumbed it open and slid the blade into the slender gap between the grate and the floorboards. Hoping that the pressure wouldn't snap the blade, I began prying the grate free. Once it was loosened enough to accommodate my fingertips I simply pulled it out and set it aside.

$\cdot \quad \cdot \quad \cdot$

I TOOK a moment to quietly remind myself that there was almost certainly nothing within this duct and definitively ascertaining that an area is free of further evidence based on thorough investigation is still a valid technique that yields viable information. That being said, I couldn't help but to hope against hope for something, for anything. I hesitantly inserted my slightly trembling hand inside the rectangular cavity. The duct had an approximate depth of ten to twelve inches and I felt a cold draft against my lightly sweating palm as I blindly felt around.

Laying upon my chest I reached deeper until I was awkwardly positioned upon the floor, practically my entire arm inside the vent and there, at the most extreme reach of my fingertips, I felt a coarse fold of fabric. After 45 or so seconds of uncomfortable contorting I managed to grasp the fabric between the fingertips of my index and middle finger. Inch by inch I began drawing it closer until I had a proper hold on it. It was some sort of hard, broad object wrapped in a rough cloth. Turning it so that it would pass through the rectangular opening I extricated the mysterious parcel. There, wrapped in heavily stained canvas, was almost certainly a book. I gingerly unfurled each corner of the canvas to reveal the cover of a heavy, seemingly handmade tome. The cover was fashioned of gray driftwood bound in a trawling net. No title nor author appeared on either cover or spine. My heart rate surged and my body thrummed with exhilaration. I stood and carried the book over to the desk where I sat and placed it before me. I opened the cover, knowing that the last person to have done the same was most assuredly Maynard years ago. Within the cover was a title page and written upon that page by an unsteady hand in thick black ink it read:

"*THE PANOMNIBUS INFINITUM*".

. . .

I'm a respectably educated man but language has always remained an elusive cypher and therefore the title meant next to nothing to me and my untrained eyes. Yet, the symbol beneath the title was unmistakably identical to that upon the cover of the journal.

I quickly began pouring through the pages which detailed the bizarre circumstances surrounding the birth of what was here referred to as the "Cenobium of the Primordial Prophecy", which appeared to be some variety of zealous denomination founded by a man named Sterling Lafayette who was, at one time, the lighthouse keeper. Incidentally, He was also the author of this unsettling scripture. It told of an abstract and alien artifact that Sterling found washed ashore, described as a conduit of sorts. An item from this point forward referred to as *"The Molybdus Articulate"*.

The apocryphal texts were scrawled by a reckless and wild hand so taken with frenzy that at times there was no cohesive order or format to the erratic pages, but rather a spalling kaleidoscopic expulsion of disparate dissertation that lay where it fell. The sheer discordant pacing of the metre in which it was written was dizzying. There were brief interludes of cognizant lucidity that felt like sanctuaries strung between hopeless vistas of raving babble. The contents spoke of Sterling's communion with the "Pure One", through the aid of the artifact, and how its cleansing embrace would consecrate those that have become "not unlike that which lurks in baleful silence". Scanning rapidly over passage after surreptitious passage, Sterling Lafayette had begun to refer to himself as "The Warden", detailing a grisly practice of self disfigurement and ritual mutilation performed during several sacred ceremonies of extreme mortification in exchange for what was here denoted as "hyper-planar boons.".

. . .

THESE CEREMONIES WERE to continue until "the flaws and faults of my corporeal flesh have been shed and wholly replaced with sacral favors, until I become compatible enough with eternity to either assimilate or foster". This book was a senseless compendium of hierarchical structure, erratic instruction and criteria pertaining to compulsory sacrifice and the unflinching dedication to an unseen malevolent entity that lies beyond and communicates through a sentient object hereby known as the Molybdus Articulate.

I was finding it increasingly difficult to make heads or tales of the information within this "Panomnibus Infinitum". Could this "Molybdus Articulate" be the item mentioned by Maynard in the journal, the very same item Benjamin Hammond has hired me to locate and retrieve? If that be the case there will no doubt be others infatuated with it, if the descriptions thus far are any indication of the influence that it truly exudes.

Roughly two thirds into the book there was placed a woefully battered gulls feather acting as a placeholder between the yellowed pages and there I found a rough charcoal sketch that occupied a whole page from top to bottom. It was an internal diagram of the lighthouse and the mechanisms that drive it. The lighthouse was as one would expect it to be, a series of ascending floors, stacked atop one another consecutively. Each floor was dedicated to fulfilling a different purpose. There were storage rooms for oil, food and water, a kitchen, guest chambers as well as the upper sleeping chamber where, historically, the lighthouse keeper called home. Above those quarters, according to the sketch, there was a machine room where the actual mechanisms would be wound by the lighthouse keeper at regular intervals to maintain a constant rotation of the beacon.

. . .

LASTLY THERE WAS the beacon housing itself at the pinnacle of the lighthouse. I glanced up from the page at the distant lighthouse, unyielding against the assault of the storm. Everything indicated that it was there I'd find the answers I sought. It suddenly occurred to me that the beacon wasn't lit, which struck me as peculiar. Had it been lit the night of my arrival? I didn't think so. The fact that the lighthouse wasn't performing it's duties was alarming given the severity of the storm rolling inland. Perhaps there simply wasn't enough maritime activity off the coast of Port Cairn to justify the expense of the oil consumed by the beacon. There were but a scant few vessels docked at the harbor when last I had seen it, after all.

The next page, as well as what remained of The Panomnibus Infinitum, was blank. I gently closed the cover and absentmindedly stared out the window and decided that I'd visit the lighthouse in the morning. For now I had a few questions that Mrs. Shoals could perhaps answer. Particularly in regards to Sterling Lafayette.

I rose from the chair and went in search of Meredith's chambers, although I'd hate to rouse her if she was indeed asleep. That poor woman seemed near catatonic last I'd laid eyes upon her. It also dawned on me that I hadn't the slightest idea where to find her chambers but I was willing to wager they'd be on the third floor, something akin to a penthouse suite, most likely. Closing the door behind me, I left room number 3 and strode down the hallway, past the kitchen and to the foot of the staircase near the foyer. The well worn planks softly moaned when they bore my weight upon them.

. . .

I CLIMBED PERHAPS twelve steps before there was a landing where the stairs switch-backed upon themselves to the left but on the right a hallway stretched away from the landing before plunging into oppressive darkness and out of sight. That was the second floor. Turning to the left I continued up the remaining 10 or so steps where they terminated at a poorly illuminated simple wooden door. There was no overt marking upon the door that distinguished it from any other door within Meridians End save for the absence of distinction. Every other door, except the front door of course, had placed upon it a brass numerical placard denoting it as guest accommodations. After a cursory inspection of the hairline gap beneath the door I concluded there was no apparent source of light beyond. I rapped my knuckles sharply against the wood and waited for any response. I knocked a second time, louder than the first and called out, "Meredith? It's Edmond. I'm terribly sorry to bother you, I know it's late and you must be exhausted but I was hoping to perhaps ask you a few questions if you'd permit me but a moment of your time."

Atop the utmost step I stood expectantly awaiting a response that never came.

A weary creak of wood sounded from somewhere beyond the door and for the briefest moment a ray of amethyst light spilled out from the gap underneath. I was growing uncomfortable and my certainty that Mrs. Shoals would be living on the third floor was faltering. That being said, there was clearly something on the other side of this door.

I hesitantly took hold of the smooth doorknob and was none too surprised to find that the door was locked. I considered leaving it be. I considered just turning around, returning to my room and turning in for the night. In hindsight that is precisely what I wish I had done but I am so often wont to disregard my common sense in favor of my uncommon curiosities.

· · ·

I HAVE WANDERED into many a corner pursuing hunches that led me exactly to where they promised, straight into trouble. So instead, I produced my pocket knife and set to shimming the latch bolt free of the doorframe. This technique wouldn't work on doors with locks of any complexity, but for this door it would suffice. After a little jiggling and a bit of probing the door gently swung inward a few inches.

Through the narrow crack I could see only darkness, and so after returning the knife to my pocket I retrieved my lighter and lit it. Cautiously, I pressed my free hand against the door and slowly pushed it further inward, allowing the firelight to quell the darkness ahead of me. Before me stretched a large and scarcely furnished room of skeletal architecture and I realized that what I had mistaken for Meredith's living quarters was in fact a broad attic space heavily cloaked in shadows.

I stepped gingerly across the threshold but left the door ajar behind me. Although the attic was vastly open the creeping darkness lurking at the boundary of the wavering firelight evoked a sense of imminent peril and an uncharacteristic claustrophobia beset me. I suddenly found myself brimming with deep antipathy regarding whatever misfortune might betide this accursed and foolhardy venture. Again I considered abandoning this pursuit until the light of day burned away that pervading unease. And yet, there was no evident source or sound reason for its presence to begin with. Alas, my pride could simply not allow me to turn back now. I pressed onward, with each step carrying me deeper into the darkness and farther from sanctuary and safe harbor.

· · ·

STREWN about me were various boxes and crates containing indeterminate possessions and furniture draped in pale canvas sheets. I squinted into the darkness for any indication of what may have been skulking around inside that disquieting chamber isolated and estranged from the comforting familiarity of light.

Although I found no ghoulish fiends lying in wait I did spy the faint outline of another door situated at the far end of the room. With great wariness I drew nearer, closing the distance whilst carefully traversing any obstacles in my path. I had been trained in how to execute a stealthy approach during my time in the military. That moment seemed to me a very appropriate time to recall that training. I'd crossed three quarters of that depthlessly sable room when the perimeters of the door ahead of me abruptly flared with lambent shafts of haunting purple light that softly pulsed in arrhythmic patterns.

The unannounced radiance startled me so drastically that I reeled midstep and nearly went careening to the floor. I fumbled with the lighter in my hand and it was only blind fortune that I managed to catch it before it struck the floorboards, incurring a burn upon my palm in the process. Standing upright once more I stared hungrily into the mesmerizing purple glow saturating the airborne particulates around the door. There was something so seductively entrancing about its nameless and amorphous warmth. I found myself inconsolably drawn towards it, awakening within me a primal attraction that begged acknowledgment. I longed for that light, ached in the most distant recesses of my psyche to embrace it and allow its magnanimous eminence to fill every fault and imperfection that has barred me from ascending beyond the fetters of human naivety.

.   .   .

THE NEXT I knew I was blinking slack into darkness, mouth agape and breathing heavily. There was a cold film of sweat that clung to me and a chill traveled up my spine that sent goose flesh spreading across the nape of my neck. My heart was racing within my chest, my pulse pounding in my ears. Panicking, I wondered how much time had passed standing there. The lighter was no longer in my hand. I dropped to my knees and frantically felt around blindly in search of it until my finger grazed the cool rectangular metallic case a foot and a half to my right. Grasping it firmly I thumbed the wheel and the flame burst to life in my hand. I immediately looked down to my watch and was both relieved and confused to find that only a few minutes had passed, and yet it felt as if I'd been locked in that ethereal embrace for aeons.

The primal urge to flee welled up within me and it was only through sheer willpower that I held fast. The door was but another ten feet further. Bolstering my resolve I steeled myself and, with clenched fist and gritted teeth, I approached.

The door itself was unremarkable. Just one of the many doors within Meridians End. I pressed my ear to the door and listened intently. From beyond the doorway I heard only silence. As quietly as possible I turned the knob and swung the door open. Before my eyes could absorb even the broadest of details within I was assailed by a cankerous and repulsive pungency, not that of rot but rather the odiferous fester of suppurating sepsis and weeping infection. Covering my nose and mouth with my unoccupied hand I held the lighter aloft before me at arms length and was astonished at what the flame revealed. Every square inch of the walls, ceiling and floor were riddled with jagged script crammed into cryptic patterns that spiraled outward and radiated into concentric circles bleeding senselessly into the next incoherent cluster.

. . .

IT WAS a fractal tapestry of unhinged hysteria that I could hardly appreciate amidst the gangrenous putrefaction that hung heavily in the air. There was a crash of thunder and the room was briefly set ablaze as lightning struck outside. My attention was immediately drawn towards the right side of this rank chamber when amidst the flash I caught a glimpse of subtle movement from out the corner of my eye. I spun, quickly orienting myself into a combative stance and held the lighter aloft. The hand that had been poorly shielding my nose darted to draw a gun that wasn't there, a gun that had been left in my own quarters below.

There, in the wavering firelight, I saw an unutterable mutagenic abomination which defied all preconceptions of benevolent providence and deific altruism. A diluvial flood of unfettered dread bound me in place, threatening to tear the precarious sinews of my psyche and sunder what quivering sanity I could still call my own. Before me, seated in a wicker wheel chair beside a small circular window overlooking the lighthouse, was an all but unidentifiable Meredith Shoals, nude and horribly distorted. She sat upright, casually leaning against the backrest with her head hung to the side, an expression somewhere between ecstasy and relief swam across her face as she moaned softly.

Yet, her limbs were broken and stretched, the mottled gray flesh around the shoulder and pelvic joints had tumefied and split revealing a squirming subdermal mass of corrupted connective tissues, a slithering weave of root like tendrils lubricated by some creamy discharge of congealing lutescent viscosity that would occasionally slop to the hardwood floor in heavy dollops. A visceral terror gripped me and held me anchored in gaping silence. The front of her abdomen was a yawning wound of septic necrosis, her rib cage stripped bare of flesh and muscle save for the yellowed nodules of subcutaneous fat that spilled out the ragged edges.

Each exposed rib had thickened into a gnarled protuberance of sallow cartilage reminiscent of arachnid appendages, jointed and articulate. Each interlaced with the next, glistening with slick moisture in the flickering firelight.

A gritty wheeze rattled from within with every sodden breath she drew and as her eyes found mine she said jovially, "Oh, Edmund. I was so terribly tight, I just about burst at the seams!", and began quietly giggling to herself, and with that laughter those cartilaginous and spindly fingers of pale striated chitin that had been weaved together over the sternum began to flex and contract asynchronously. As they did that hypnotic pulsing purple glow seeped through the negative spaces from the hidden recesses of her chest cavity, illuminating Meredith's grinning face from below and casting malignant shadows of writhing knot work upon the scripture riddled walls and ceiling.

With a heavy thud Meredith's arms struck the floor as the dense nest of snaking tendrils at the shoulders seemed to unravel, spilling a fresh gout of that repugnant ichor down the sides of the chair. The index finger of her left hand curled and beckoned me coquettishly from where her arm had settled upon the floorboards. A muffled insectile chittering thrummed beneath those twisted and malformed ribs. Slowly they splayed themselves outward and the room was bathed in otherworldly purple light as a cloud of droning corpse flies burst forth from within.

A chilling sound rose up in the darkness, shrill and guttural and only later did I realize that it was the sound of my own screaming. A deep and primal necessity to flee urged me to break my stillness. I spun on my heel and sprinted through the doorway, striking my shoulder on the doorframe in my panic. I frantically ran through the open attic in complete darkness, my only means of navigating was the low light filtering through the far door I'd left ajar.

.   .   .

MY FOOT STRUCK some heavy object as I fled that sent me crashing
to the floor. I scrambled back to my feet and continued my mad
dash of self preservation. Bolting through the door I slammed it
shut behind me and peeled down the stairs, taking them two at a
time. Once I was back on the ground floor I made directly for my
room. I had no intention of lingering another moment in Meridian's End. I burst through my door and rapidly gathered what little
personal effects I had. Grabbing my revolver I hesitated only long
enough to affix the holster to myself before heading towards the
entryway and out of that profane and accursed inn. Within
seconds of stepping outside I was drenched by the torrential
downpour.

PART V - THE LIGHTHOUSE

It was only once there were several hundred feet between myself and Meridian's End that I slowed to a halt. Dropping to my knees in the sand I struggled to catch my breath as my feckless mind attempted to make sense of Meredith's nauseating display. There resides a place deep within all of us, a place where we process the endless information that is filtered through our primitive senses and determines the validity of that input. What I had just experienced seemed far too large for that place to accommodate and was rejected over and over again. Like some latent defense mechanism my faculties outright refused to accept that what had transpired in that attic was possible because to do so would rend my mind into madness. I sat there upon my knees in the sand, mouth agape and staring vacuously off into the tumultuous expanse of ocean as the rain and wind whipped around me. After a time I emerged from my fugue and turned my attention to the lighthouse.

.   .   .

I HARDLY REGISTERED the fact that there was now a faint source of light gently illuminating a section of the base. Rising to my feet I blinked the rain from my eyes and brushed the damp sand from my palms before making for the lighthouse which was but a mere 500 feet or so away.

The towering lighthouse painted a formidable picture cast against the seething black skyline with the sea churning foam around the jagged stone plinth it perched upon. Drawing near I could see a narrow rocky path that wend its way from the shore outward towards the lighthouse. It wasn't difficult to imagine this thin strip of stone being swallowed beneath the surf when the tides rolled in. I continued with haste onto the path and was part way across when a large wave broke against the outer stone, crashing into me and nearly carrying me over the far side into the black waters that would have no doubt dragged me under to either drown or be mercilessly dashed against the rocks.

Clambering to my feet I dashed across the remaining distance before slowing my advance. Ahead of me, stretching into the incensed sky above, was the lighthouse. After the events of the evening I found myself desperately wanting for fortitude and yet the answer to every question I'd amassed lay just ahead. The light I had spied from shore turned out to be a hooded lantern hung from a hook to the left of the entry door to the lighthouse. I was certainly not alone. I squatted down and observed the door for a few moments but to no avail. Whoever else occupied this island was surely within, sheltering themselves from the storm. I crept closer, drawing my revolver as I did.

I AM many things but a fool isn't one of them. If the incident in Meridian's End had taught me anything it was that I feel far more at ease with my firearm close at hand. The landscape between the door and myself was mostly scarce save for the occasional patch of tall, hardy grass that had managed to take root among the stone. Utilizing these for cover I slipped from one grassy clump to the next. I had all but reached the door when it began to swing inward, the hinges grating against themselves even among the raging storm.

Those dormant instincts, remnants from the war, flared to life and before I had any say in the matter I'd dropped flat onto my belly among the grass. From in between the blades I could see two figures exiting the lighthouse, one tall and lanky whose face was obscured by a generous cowl and the other shorter and vaguely hunched forward who I immediately recognized as being Cliff, the older gentleman I'd spoken to on the docks.

They strode a short way from the door before Cliff stopped and turned towards the other individual. The hooded figure addressed Cliff and said,

"Assemble the Acolytes. Brother Abernathy has achieved Symbiosis and has begun his preparatory isolation. The time has come to present him before the Pure One. Tell the others that the Ritual of Winding will commence later this evening. Pray his sacrifice be looked upon with favor." His words were all but washed away by the frenzied wind and rain.

Cliff seemed to bow his head slightly in a display of supplication before replying, "At once, sir. I hope ya don't think this too forward of me but do ya suppose it possible that I might attend tonight's ceremony? I do so long for communion, sir."

.　.　.

THE CLOAKED man took a step closer to Cliff and placed a hand on his shoulder before speaking again, "Brother Clifford, your devotion is inspiring, your faith is without falter. Assemble the others. Ferry them along the coast and anchor your vessel nearby. You will stand alongside us as Brother Abernathy prostrates himself before the Molybdus Articulate."

Cliff, eyes still cast downward, deepened his bow before turning about and hurriedly trot across the stone away from the lighthouse and towards the only place of egress on this rocky outcropping. The other man stood unmoving amidst the downpour and looked on as Cliff departed. Once out of sight the figure lingered a minute longer before retreating within the lighthouse once more.

I remained prone, thoroughly drenched and shivering against the cold ground, weighing my limited options and considering how to best proceed. I'd come this far, I reasoned, endured incalculably abstruse manifestations of traumatic torment and twisted abyssal aberrations that offend the very foundation of sacral firmament. I had witnessed things that fundamentally and permanently changed me. I remembered feeling that same sensation on the night I killed for the first time during the war. You cannot unsee, you cannot undo, you cannot unknow. I found myself aching, physically, palpably aching, aching to be inside that lighthouse. I was going to see this to the end. Rising from the stone I purposely strode to the door and tried the handle. Finding it unlocked I pushed the door open and stepped inside, swinging it shut behind me quietly.

THE INTERIOR WAS SATURATED in velvety dark obscurity and once the door had latched behind me I couldn't see a thing. Holstering my revolver I fetched the lighter from my pocket once more. I was acutely aware of the fact that I wasn't alone within this lighthouse and as my eyes adjusted to the firelight they flitted anxiously around the room, hunting for any indication of the man's presence. Neatly tucked against the interior stone wall were many crates and barrels, stacked categorically and with intent. In the center of this circular chamber was a tight metallic staircase spiraling around a central pole that rose approximately twenty feet before disappearing into the chamber above this one and, I surmised, would likely ascend through the entirety of the lighthouse.

I was thoroughly soaked and the unforgiving stone of the lighthouse resulted in the ambient temperature being uncomfortably cool. I could have searched through the crates and the barrels seeking this eldritch artifact, this "Molybdus Articulate", and yet there was no need. I could feel it. As difficult as that may be to understand it is far more difficult to describe such an abstract sensation with something so primitive as language. There was a presence, unseen and unobtrusive, but gently guiding me nonetheless, ushering me with eager anticipation.

My consciousness felt crowded, not as if my own were being shunted aside but rather as if something had seeped into the empty places within my own mind, inhabiting the hollow recesses that stretch between one thought and the next. As strange and as alien as this sensation was I suddenly found myself feeling somehow more whole than I had ever felt before. I experienced a resounding revelation, that I was brought into this world wanting.

. . .

WE WERE all of us born incomplete and we spend our sad lives in ignorance, squabbling and consuming and trying in hopeless futility to unwittingly stumble upon the that which will fill our inherent void. There, in that dismal lighthouse, I stood upon the precipice of perfection and the chill that had crept into my aching bones was gradually replaced with a softly thrumming warmth. I knew that this was but a meager sample of what unknowable wonders awaited me above.

Navigating in the direction of the spiral staircase I happened upon a queer apparatus affixed to a large metallic drum whose purpose was not immediately apparent but pausing briefly to further inspect this contraption I derived that the drum was a reservoir for oil and the adjacent device was a hydraulic pump, likely used to fuel the beacon. I found it curious that it would be so far from the top of the lighthouse until it dawned on me that hauling oil up all those stairs was less than an ideal solution. Regardless, I pressed on and took my first step upon the weathered stairs that would guide me to my ultimate destination.

Climbing upward I passed from the lower chamber into the next, my lighter held aloft before me. There was an unpleasant aroma in the room of vegetative rot and mildew and as I peered around I saw that I was within a small, utilitarian kitchen/dining space. To my left stood a rough wooden table with a pair of mismatching chairs to either side. On the round tabletop sat a single tin plate where the slowly decaying remnants of a meal remained untouched. I determined the kitchen and adjacent dining area were long in disuse.

THE SALT RUSTED staircase led upward still, another twenty feet or so before transitioning into the next floor. As I looked towards the entryway above a gentle wave of ephemeral periwinkle light washed over the stairs, not unlike that I'd seen in my dreams and yet it seemed somehow softer, diffused, reminiscent of the manner in which light reflects off water. I had hardly begun to contemplate the implications of that distant glow when from the floor above came quietly cascading a lilting cadence of incognizant warbling, somewhere between chanting and chittering and the very sound set my skin crawling.

Slowly ascending the steps I withdrew my Colt from its holster once again. Firing the revolver was a last resort as doing so would certainly reveal my presence and position but I felt bolstered in my resolve for having it in hand. As I approached the next landing the warbling grew softer, muddled with incoherent whispers. I heard the shuffling of feet and the slithering of chains against stone. Cautiously, I laid my fingers on the lip of the landing and craned my head upward so that my line of sight was level with the floor.

The ground was awash with rippling waves of gossamer violet light spilling from floors farther above and as my eyes turned towards the ceiling of this chamber I saw that the floor above this one was not of stone as the rest had been but was fashioned instead of steel grate. The frantic whispers rose again and my eyes darted to the right side of this chamber where there was but a single austere cot, the only item furnishing this floor. There beside the cot was a lone figure squat upon their haunches, back turned and face pressed against the wall. The purple light danced across their exposed back and glinted mutely off the heavy steel chain affixed to their right ankle.

. . .

FROM WHAT FLESH was visible I could see they were riddled with gaping wounds and thick ropy scar tissue that tore across the bare back in jagged swathes. Although mildly illuminated from above the figure was mostly obscured in darkness and these minor details were only perceptible when trace amounts of that eerie light fell across them. I gingerly climbed the few stairs that remained and silently took a step in their direction. Without warning, the individual began to tremble and as tremors raced through their body that withering warble rose once more. In the dim light I watched as long vertical slabs of pale flesh along either side of their flanks retracted towards the spine, exposing slick muscle tissue bristling with coarse chitinous protuberances.

What little courage had carried me that far promptly dissolved and as I was about to flee those naked muscular striations rapidly slid across one another with mucosal ease producing a reverberant droning thrum that filled the chamber. The shrill vibratory resonance of the stridulation assaulted my senses with such profound intensity that I clapped my hands over my ears as my knees gave out and I fell to the ground. I crawled across the stone floor, dragging myself forward with my elbows until I dropped onto the stairs. There, I curled myself into a fetal ball, covering my ears and keeping my eyes tightly closed for fear of them rupturing.

Seconds felt like hours as I helplessly lay there clawing at my ears, weeping in agony and praying for reprieve. When the droning finally subsided a relief washed over me unlike any I had ever experienced and I simply remained there breathing heavily. The silence felt oppressive in the aftermath. Then the chains rattled above and suddenly I recalled what grave danger I was in. I admit it was this very moment that I'd had enough. I was thoroughly finished with this entire venture.

· · ·

"To hell with Hammond, and to hell with the Molybdus Articulate. There was no amount of curiosity or compensation that would ever make any of this worthwhile," I thought bitterly.

Bracing myself against the railing for support I slowly stood and realized that I had dropped my revolver when I clasped my ears. To hell with that as well. I descended three steps when the silence was broken as a meek feminine voice issued from above, "Eddy...Eddy, is that you?"

I froze in place. A cold sweat erupted across my brow and my breath caught in my throat. It may have been twenty years since I last heard it but a man doesn't forget his mother's voice.

"Please, Eddy. Don't leave me like this. I'm cold and I'm scared."

Somewhere in the coiled and clandestine depths of my mind, on the calm dark waters of the psyche, the frayed tether attached to my sanity snapped, setting it adrift, to drift and drift...

The rational part of my mind was acutely aware that the last time I'd seen my mother was the day I left for the war. She died in 1918 when the cancer took her. However, the rational part of my mind had recently been greatly reduced and as I stared vacantly into the darkness below I called out weakly, "Mom?".

The only response I received was the sound of heavy sobbing. Sluggishly I turned about and, with my hand trailing along the railing, I climbed back up. Re-entering the chamber I turned and there she was, my mother, as if she had never stopped aging. Her brunette hair now streaked with gray, her compassionate hazel eyes, the small crescent scar above her left eyebrow, every detail so completely and entirely hers. She sat beside the cot, knees tucked beneath her chin, gently rocking as she cried.

. . .

DISTANTLY I HEARD myself say "Mom, you're dead. What are you doing here?"

THE ROCKING STOPPED as she looked up at me, doing her best to conceal her nakedness, as a modest woman does.

SHE REPLIED, "It's this place, Emmy. We've been here so long. You can't trust the things you see here."

FURIOUSLY, I reiterated, "You died alone while I was fighting at the Somme! What are you doing here!"

AT MY OUTBURST she pulled her legs in closer to her chest and whimpered, "Listen to yourself, Emmett. There never was a war."

"STOP," I said breathlessly.

"THINK, try and remember how long you've been here. Please, I need you here, now, with me, Emmett!"

I CLUTCHED the sides of my head and bellowed, "STOP CALLING ME THAT!"

. . .

MY FACE WENT slack and my arms dropped to my sides where they swung limply. Of course I knew how long I'd been there. I'd arrived in town earlier that day. Well, that didn't make any sense. Why didn't it make sense? Because I remembered a picnic on the beach. A beach beside a lighthouse. This lighthouse. A picnic with my mother on my eighteenth birthday. I remember we had to move the blanket back because the tide was coming in. But I was in town on a job. What was my job? Traveling salesman, perhaps, but that didn't sound right. I tried to recall detailed accounts of the war but all the faces were vague, featureless, their names escaped me. My memories felt like looping dream sequences.

I was getting lightheaded. My left arm itched fiercely but it was all so far away. If my mother was there then was the rest of my family? I had a younger brother, didn't I? Yes, his name was Tommy. But Tommy died a long time ago. My head was spinning. My father must have died during the war. But there never was a war, was there? There was never a job. Just the warm glow of the Molybdus Articulate and the few things fortunate enough to reside within it. The itching in my arm had turned into a searing heat. The heat grew unbearable, drowning out everything else as my fingertips felt like they were melting away.

I cried out in pain and blinked my eyes and as I did so I found myself standing exactly where I had been, only now my mother was gone. I was nauseous, drenched in cold sweat and hyperventilating. Terror clawed its icy hands along my spine. I glanced over to see the chained individual hunched beside me, my arm stuffed inside it's distended maw up to the elbow as cruelly serrated mandibles pierced my skin and pulled my arm deeper within. I gasped involuntarily as one of the mandible's barbed tips snagged upon a tendon, tugging the elastic tissue like a marionette string.

. . .

FROM BETWEEN LONG, greasy strands of thin black hair a pair of bulbous pale lavender eyes flit up to meet my gaze and a deep insectile chittering emanated from within its chest. I screamed and wrenched my arm, drawing the creature with me as its throat constricted around my forearm. I reached up with my right hand and thrust my thumb into one of the eye sockets. My thumb squelched between the gelatinous orb and the tensing muscle. The eye bulged outward as I forced my thumb deeper, hooking it behind the eye and prying it free where it dangled from a clustered bundle of nerves.

The figure attempted to scream and as it did so I tore my arm free, seizing the opportunity. Unfortunately for me, I anticipated more resistance than I was met with and the momentum carried me backwards where I partially stepped upon my revolver. My foot snapped sharply to the side as I felt the bone split in my ankle. I yelped and fell prone upon my back as waves of throbbing pain radiated up my leg. That abomination threw its head back, releasing an ear piercing trill that felt as though it was originating from within my own skull. I arched my back at the sudden spike of agony, tensing against the onslaught of that unearthly chirping. As I laid there writhing the ghoulish figure pounced upon me.

It had pinned my arms beneath its knees as it straddled my chest, firmly planting its hands on either side of my head. The entire face below the eyes was a churning hole of flexing tissue and masticating teeth between those devastating mandibles. It leaned forward and its face contorted as it began to heave violently, a horribly wet sound of suction rising from within its chest. I struggled against the overwhelming strength of this aberrant miscreation, attempting to free my arms. It continued retching, spreading its mouth open wide to reveal a large, hooked ebony beak protruding from the rear of its raw throat.

· · ·

With each heave the cephalopodic beak was forcefully thrust forward until the jagged tip emerged and the beak filled the entirety of the mouth. The creature reared back and lunged forward to strike my throat and as it did so I met it halfway with a well placed headbutt. It wasn't much but it was enough to cause what I later learned to be "Brother Abernathy" to momentarily release the pressure on my right arm. I swiftly grabbed my revolver and before that heinous monstrosity could recover, I thumbed back the hammer and fired. The muzzle flash briefly filled the room with blinding light as the bullet slammed through the creature's beak, blowing out the rear of its skull and yet it still writhed and shrieked atop me.

I fired again, and again, and again. I fired until it grew still, and then I fired once more. My ears rang and the chamber grew thick with smoke and the scent of spent powder. I began crawling out from beneath Abernathy as I heard footsteps hurriedly descending the steel stairs from above. My arm was already in motion, swinging the revolver towards the stairs when there was an incredible impact against the side of my head, a brief flash of phosphorus white, and then blackest serenity.

PART VI - THE MOLYBDUS ARTICULATE

Without form or awareness I drifted among an ocean of absolute nothingness. Then there was warmth and with that warmth there came awareness. Thoughtless and pure, I existed indefinitely. Then, from aeons afar, came a soft popping accompanied by lights that briefly flared among the perpetual void and I thought "I am witnessing the birth of stars". With that singular thought there came form and I was carried along the gentle current of eternity. Louder popping and brighter light, closer than before and with that realization there was time. Garbled vocalizations, muted and muddled, issued from all around. There came a great roaring from overhead and suddenly there was direction.

GRADUALLY THE MUFFLED sounds sharpened and intensified. I could feel solidity beneath me. Anguished wailing and concussive detonations punctuated the frenetic chaos. The roaring was returning and as my eyes fluttered open I looked upward into a gray sky above as a Fokker Fighter tore across the clouds, spraying rounds indiscriminately as tracers left trailing tendrils of smoke to hang in the air. Holding my helmet firmly against my head I clambered to my feet. My team lay scattered about me, broken and mangled, their vacant eyes staring out from ruined faces. The air was thick with dust and black smoke from fires raging nearby.

I pressed myself against the sandbags stacked along the wall of the trench and bandaged my arm which sustained some damage in the blast that killed my team. I had to find the rest of my squad. I began limping my way through the trenches. The sky grew dark as night fell, fires burned and men screamed as explosions rocked the earth. Gunfire rattled from every direction. There was terror and panic and the trenches turned and split and branched outward in unrecognizably complex patterns, a labyrinth of dirt and wood littered with the detritus of mutilated corpses. As the night stretched on the urgency swelled until I was running and running and running. The smoke was dense and it had been hours since I'd seen another living man. I was alone there with the dead, sprinting through an endlessly long grave. Unbeknownst to me the screaming had faded along with the gunfire and silence had filled the trenches.

I pressed onward, choking through the fog of billowing smoke, hardly able to perceive anything but vague shapes before me. All was still and quiet save for the crackling of the fires. Trudging forward there rose a discordant cacophony of hissing whispers, omnipresent and directionless. I slowed to a steady trot, breathing raggedly, weaving through the truncated cadavers and severed limbs of good and brave men. The whispering swelled into a low rolling chant as I passed corpses spilling viscera, skulls caved and flesh stripped from bone.

I tried to look away but the reluctant deceased were everywhere, sprawling across the blood sodden earth, piled carelessly atop one another. Their faces wracked with anguish and fear and looking on I realized with brimming horror that their pale lips moved in unison. The myriad dead sang as one:

"HERALD, HARBINGER, HOST, HERALD, HARBINGER, HOST, HERALD, HARBINGER, HOST..."

I FELT a scream climb its way up my throat and explode from out my mouth. I tried to run but found myself wading through rousing bodies, frantically scaling insurmountable mounds of restlessly squirming undead, recently risen from repose. They clawed and raked with hooked and stiffened fingers as the chanting quickened, each word punctuated with power and purpose:

"HERALD! HARBINGER! HOST!"

THERE WAS NO ESCAPE, the dead were without number. I feverishly crawled and the corpses dragged me down deeper as they sang louder and louder until I turned my face to the inflamed purple sky and screamed in vain futility. The chanting reached a deafening crescendo and just as I was being swallowed beneath the stinking corpses the sky above crackled with cruel lightning arcing through it, revealing a colossal silhouette concealed among the clouds.

"HERALD! HARBINGER! HOST!"

.   .   .

GROGGILY I CAME TO CONSCIOUSNESS, the chanting continuing from somewhere above. My head was pounding and the left side of my face was sticky with congealing blood. I tentatively probed the area to find a deep and very tender laceration. There was a single candle burning beside the spiral staircase which didn't provide a great deal of light but was sufficient for me to determine that I was still in the chamber, although there was no longer that nascent violet glow. I was on the cot and the chain was shackled to the ankle that wasn't broken. My possessions had been stripped from my person with the exception of my pants although my pockets were emptied. My sporadic thoughts were hazy and disorganized and it was likely that I had a concussion.

The entirety of my body screamed in defiance of the variety of lingering pains. I looked to my left arm, the arm that had been unceremoniously stuffed inside the slavering jaws of Abernathy. My forearm was raw and rife with weeping pustules where the flesh had been corroded away by caustic digestive acid. My hand was devastated. The last three fingers were nothing more than ragged stumps with staggering lengths of splintered bone protruding from the pulverized meat. The rest of the hand wasn't so easy to look at either. What the beak hadn't taken entirely it had taken in pieces and I was missing significant hunks of flesh, where tendons and subdermal tissue were flayed open and exposed. Looking upon it made my stomach turn and I rolled to the side before projecting vomit on the stone floor, the straining efforts involved causing my head to spin and I proceeded to vomit again.

"HERALD, HARBINGER, HOST, HERALD..."

.   .   .

I LOOKED UPWARD to the incessant sound of the chanting, hopelessly wishing that whoever was up there would stop. My head was splitting in drumming waves that promised to fracture my skull, If it wasn't already.

A pair of footsteps began purposely descending the stairs. I simply laid back on the cot and waited. My ankle was shattered, my skull bludgeoned and my arm stripped bare. I was in no condition to put up a fight and frankly, at this point I didn't much care to. Two hooded figures stepped onto the landing and approached. One held what appeared to be my revolver and stopped a few feet shy while the other stepped forward, producing a key and unlocked the shackle. I spat a thick wad of saliva at the feet of the far individual who promptly strode forward, grabbed the hair on the back of my head and smashed the steel butt of the Colt into my teeth three successive times. With the first staggering blow the flesh of my lips split against my teeth. The second caved my front teeth inward, shattering some while others ripped wholly through the gums. The final blow mashed my mangled lips into the jagged serrations of my broken teeth, piercing and slashing them to grisly ribbons.

I coughed as blood filled my mouth and ran down my chest in warm rivulets. Each hooded figure took one of my arms in theirs and hoisted me to my feet. As my broken ankle tried to support the weight of my body I felt the shards of bone grate sharply against one another and I cried out as my knees buckled. The two individuals caught me and started carrying me towards the stairs as my head hung limply, spilling heavy drops of blood to the stone below.

I WAS BROUGHT straight through the next chamber. As we continued ascending the chanting grew closer, always the same "Herald, Harbinger, Host". It never wavered nor faltered. Right before we reached the following floor I vomited once again, mostly yellow bile streaked with blood. Here the stairs terminated and we stepped into a chamber illuminated with oil lanterns. Eight other figures stood in a circle against the inner wall, all dressed in identical burlap cloaks with hoods drawn up. Below their hoods their faces were hidden beneath simple masks of smooth driftwood and in perfect unison they zealously chanted, "Herald! Harbinger! Host!".

On the far side of the room there was a brief staircase leading upward and to the left of that a recess set into the wall housing some piece of machinery. The tallest figure stepped forward raising a hand that cued the others to immediately fall silent. This person strode across the chamber before stopping in front of me, the other two men still holding me aloft. The individual withdrew their hood and doffed the mask. Standing before me was none other than Benjamin Hammond.

"Mr. Jameson, how wonderful it is to see you again. You seem to be a little worse for wear but I dare say you'll pull through." He smiled pleasantly revealing those unsettling teeth crammed into neat little rows.

One of the men holding me upright seized a handful of my hair and jerked my head back so I was looking into Hammonds eyes.

I QUERIED WEAKLY, "WHAT the hell is going on here, Hammond?"

. . .

"Oh, dear boy, I'm afraid you may be in over your head. You've arrived early but, as my father was wont to say, if you're on time then you're late. You are most welcome."

From within the folds of his cloak he produced the journal, absentmindedly flipping through the pages before sighing as he continued, "I must thank you for returning this. It's indescribably dear to me. I suppose we're beyond these facades and charades now. Allow me, if you will, the opportunity to formally introduce myself. My name is Maynard Mathers, although these fine individuals address me as Warden Mathers." He spoke this last bit while gesturing to the others situated around the room.

I was reeling, trying to make any sense of this. I shook my disoriented head and asked, "Why hire me to find something you've already got, why the ruse?"

Maynard ran his spindly fingers through what thin wisps of hair remained atop his jaundiced head before replying, "The truth is, Edmond, none of this has anything to do with the Molybdus Articulate. The Articulate is merely a means of communion." He leaned in uncomfortably close before whispering into my ear, "This is about you, Edmond." He withdrew again before turning to address the chamber. "You see, the Articulate has the potential to be a great many wonderful things. It can bestow blessed gifts, like in the instance of Meredith or of our late Brother Abernathy, whom you cast into the void prematurely. It can act as a beacon, guiding wayward souls to seek it's cleansing light, such as that unfortunate automobile accident you suffered and the visions leading up to it." He turned to face me again wearing a wry grin beneath those cold, yellowed eyes.

· · ·

How could he possibly know about that? Even if it wasn't a dream I was alone in my Plymouth traveling 60 miles per hour down a barren stretch of road in the dead of night. My face must have betrayed my inner thoughts as Maynard smiled once more and divulged, "I know what the Molybdus Articulate knows, Edmond. That is my duty as Warden. It is also my duty to know the desire of that which lies beyond the Articulate, and what our baleful benefactor desires, Edmond, is you."

This was pure, unadulterated raving madness. Nothing this man was saying explained anything whatsoever and, if anything, it served only to further convolute this tangled narrative.

"What lies beyond the Articulate, Mathers, and why would it want me?"

He studied me intently for a moment before replying, "It's not my place to question the will, only to hear it. It asked for you by name. Fortunately for me, you are quite capable in your profession. I merely had to hire you under false pretenses. I'm not gloating, mind you, and I do hope you'll forgive my deception, Edmond. Despite current circumstances I am impressed with your aptitude and, if you don't mind my saying so, I've grown rather fond of you."

Another wave of nausea washed over me and I only just managed to stifle the urge to retch. I looked at Mathers and calmly replied, "With all due respect, Maynard, thoroughly fuck yourself. Let's get this over with."

· · ·

HE LOOKED at me with what was clearly pity, sighed again and said, "The Molybdus Articulate illuminates all things obscured by darkness. You'll understand soon enough." He turned his head, addressing the masked figure to my left, "Carry him up and prepare him to receive the light."

I WAS SILENTLY FUMING, enraged with Maynard but equally so with myself. How could I have allowed myself to be so easily duped. I scolded my goddamned hubris. The two men carried me to the flight of stairs and upward. This was the beacon proper, a small room encased in glass with a narrow grate catwalk around the outside. Beyond the lighthouse the storm had abated and the waters had calmed somewhat. The whole of Port Cairn lay sprawling before me. I could see Cliff's ship anchored far below. I considered breaking free and throwing myself over the edge purely out of spite and yet my eyes were insatiably drawn to the center of the room.

There stood an oddly modified variation of the beacon. The refractive concave disk still remained atop the cogs and gears that propel its rotation but the source of light itself had been removed. In its stead there was a heavy black canvas cloth draped over an object roughly the size and shape of a bell jar. Looking upon it wave after wave of undulating warmth passed over me, through me. All the pain melted away and that aching sensation of longing returned. I closed my eyes, saturated in the primordial powers exuded here. The inside of my eyelids were ablaze with rich purple light, and there, in the center of it all, an infinitesimally small bead of searing radiance pulsing irregularly, as if communicating. I gasped and opened my eyes, struggling against my captives. I hungered for it, I've never wanted for anything more.

·   ·   ·

Promises of salvation resided within each passing wave and the intermittent gaps between every pulse stretched on indefinitely as I eagerly awaited the arrival of the next.

The men laughed at my feeble resistance as they dragged me to a bizarre wrought iron post that stood roughly seven feet tall. Two-thirds of the way up the post there was a cross beam that ran perpendicular to the main post and on each side of this cross beam extended another beam upward and slightly canted outward. I couldn't place it immediately but that malevolent sculpture was uncomfortably familiar to me. Suddenly I recognized it. It was the exact same shape as the symbol etched into the cover of Maynard's journal. What I had originally mistook for a trident was in fact the warped interpretation of a crucifix.

I was pressed against the post and a leather strap was affixed around my throat, then my arms were raised and my upper arms were bound to the cross beam. My hands were brought up and pressed against the canted beams where they were strapped in at the wrist. Lastly, my feet were bound to the post around the ankles where one of the men took great pleasure in further crushing my broken bones. I growled against the explosive pain, spraying spittle and blood from my sundered mouth. They then turned and retreated back down the stairs.

I remained there, breathing deeply, slick with sweat and tacky blood, waiting for whatever would come next. While I waited I closed my eyes and basked in that glow. I pondered what perilous vistas of unfettered possibility might await beyond that black canvas veil. I held no illusions of leaving this lighthouse alive. In the past few daunting days I'd undergone an unforeseen metamorphosis. I could no longer be concerned with concepts as mundane as corporeal preservation. This had transcended the tedious trivialities of flesh and broached the subject of eternity. I had become the subject of eternity.

. . .

I$_{T WAS THERE}$, within that lighthouse, that I would peel away the finite pall of impermanence, one fold of damp meat at a time till I lay bare beneath the firmament forever, no longer set apart by barriers of bone and breath but rather absorbed into the cosmic amalgamate, free of matter to churn among the infinite expanse of true immortality!

C$_{HANTING ROSE FROM BENEATH}$, strange and unearthly, words no human had ever uttered before. There was a sound of heavy machinery slowly turning as Maynard stepped into the chamber. I watched him with frothing anticipation as he approached the Molybdus Articulate. Maynard stopped beside it and turned to me. He was grave of demeanor, a fervent zeal ablaze amidst the madness of his eyes.

"B$_{Y THIS TIME TOMORROW}$, time will have ceased to exist."

E$_{VERYTHING THAT HAD TRANSPIRED}$, leading up to and including this moment suddenly and immediately seemed so comically absurd and, while I watched Maynard extend a thin arm towards the veil, I began to laugh, barking and belting hysterically until tears filled my vision and my guts knotted and still I laughed and laughed.

HE REACHED FORWARD and slowly dragged the cloth away just as the base of the beacon began to turn. There, affixed in space yet turning in time with the beacon, was a fist sized object of impossible description, although I will try. The Molybdus Articulate was both roughly hewn and intricately refined, as though intentionally so as to be unassuming. Its irregular surface was of deepest sable iridescence but as it turned there appeared to be translucent properties and when the light struck the irregular facets the Articulate multiplied and magnified, stretching and scattering, careening and coalescing. It seemed to breathe, expanding and contracting as mind bending non-Euclidean geometry rippled across its intermittently scintillating surface. All at once it stopped moving. The machinery slammed to a halt as steel ground against steel and smoke poured up from below.

Maynard swore and swiftly rushed down the steps but I'd never taken my eyes off the Articulate. A crack spiderwebbed across its pitted surface, spreading along the perfectly imperfect ridges. Where these cracks ran puerperal light seeped out and the individual fragments began to slowly unfurl. Viridescent particles drifted upward from the top and the bottom became a viscous fluid, dripping molten amber droplets that fell but a few inches before becoming static, fixed in place before lazily drifting around the primary body of the Articulate like strange satellites.

Meticulously and systematically the Molybdus Articulate was disassembling itself, splitting and dissolving, fracturing and evaporating until a prismatic nebula of debris hung in silent suspension slowly revolving around a radiant mote of pure purple light. At first I'd thought it finished with its spectacular display but as I looked onward I saw that the dust was gradually being drawn together, forming dense spheres of varying size and color, and these too were drawn towards others where they'd softly collide and meld seamlessly together.

· · ·

A DESIGN WAS TAKING shape around this potent mote of light.
When all was finished a ring of glassy black stone, perhaps six
inches in diameter, remained steadily rotating on a vertical axis
around the pinprick of amethyst light which rested precisely in
the center of the ring.

I was enraptured, mesmerized with the prospect of what
resplendent worlds might reside therein. The beacon housing was
now abuzz with humming energy and I could feel the very mole-
cules of my being quicken in the presence of such immeasurable
power. Bursting waves of celestial light poured from the windows
of that room, bathing the world below in baptismal brilliance. I
laughed and I wept and time stretched on indefinitely as I stared
into the pulsating heart of the Articulate. From some far off place I
could hear the tormented cries and torturous suffering of those
below. The black ring made one final rotation before coming to a
halt in my direction.

From my perspective I was looking through the center of the
ring at the majority of Port Cairn beyond the energetic spore of
blinding lavender light. The light appeared to dim slightly, and
then grew dimmer still and with every muting of that haunting
glow my heart burned for its return. Step by step, the light became
incrementally softer before flickering out entirely and at the exact
moment the light was snuffed out an explosive wave of latent
energy made manifest radiated outward from the center of the
ring, tearing through me and vaporizing the windows encircling
the beacon. The blast struck with such violent concussive force
that I was all but sundered entirely as my left eardrum burst.
Dazed, I hung limp, held aloft by the bindings, a tinny ringing
echoing in my head.

· · ·

THE ROOM SWAM and my vision was tinged with red as blood welled into my eyes and trickled from my nostrils. Through blurry eyes I saw the spreading pool of crimson blood amassing around the base of the crucifix. The shrieking whine in my ears faded to the muted roar of my rampaging heart, struggling to maintain. With every breath my chest seized and spasmed in convulsive pain as I realized my lung had collapsed. I wasn't able to draw enough oxygen and between the hemorrhaging and a slow but certain asphyxiation the color drained from my vision and the dreaded black began to creep into my periphery.

Yet, in spite of all my failing and fading faculties, I could feel an insistence that refused to be ignored. The Molybdus Articulate was beyond these fleeting moments of finality and couldn't be inconvenienced by something so paltry as death. With the depleted and wilting vestiges of my life force, with what improbable dregs remained, I raised my head and peered through the Articulate at the town of Port Cairn beyond.

For reasons beyond me I found myself, in that moment, inexplicably struck with a nagging curiosity. If Benjamin Hammond was in fact Maynard Mathers then who in the hell had created that incredibly detailed painting of the ship lost at sea? Had it been Mathers? Looking over the seaside town framed within that extra dimensional black ring as the lifeblood drained from my traumatically ravaged body, the painting aptly titled "The Maelstrom" was so demonstrably redundant and yet I couldn't help but recollect the flawless execution. The artist had precisely captured a static image in layers of paint and willed it come to life when looked upon. Until that day I had never before been moved by art but that painting stirred within me a sympathetic exchange of intimate sensations.

. . .

THE ARTIST HAD MANIFESTED peril and fear and mortality, not only in paint but also in me through the conduit of his creation. Staring through the thrumming Molybdus Articulate I postulated that everything was nothing more than a painting, merely infinite layers of paint upon the fabric of reality to create a cohesive image of the universe as we perceive it, manifesting emotions within us as we experience it for ourselves.

If that be the case then those layers of paint that defined the portion of Port Cairn residing within the boundaries of the black ring began to separate and run and I watched as the fundamental foundation of the third dimension was stripped away before my eyes. All things outside the ring remained unchanged while the center dissolved as details blurred and depth decayed, images bleeding together until all was flat and featureless. The center of the Molybdus Articulate was without dimension whatsoever. I wheezed shallowly and as the encroaching darkness closed in I saw a distant speck of purple light amidst that hollow emptiness fast approaching.

My consciousness left me then, elusively slipping from my mortal grasp, not to be swept away beneath the roiling undertow of primordial slurry awaiting eventual dissolution and inevitable reconstitution, but rather condensed and cradled, drawn into and beyond the unconquerable gates of the Molybdus Articulate. I breached a liminal threshold where all corporeal solidity dissolved and we were absorbed into the tattered and frayed fabric of spacetime, no longer a fragmented object resting upon that boundless weave but an osmotic singularity saturating the very sutures and seams. We split and scattered and pulsed along those arterial filaments and charged leylines, a frenetic current carrying us to the farthest reaches of conception and there, on the desolate outskirts of creation, we answered its summons.

. . .

No more were we baffled by the convoluted illusion of individualism. There was only the duality between all that was and all that was not. We had been delivered unto the precipice of a fathomless boundary where any that exist beyond exist in the vacuous lacuna of exile, shunned outside the purview of dimensional recognition. We had become all that was and before us, lurking in baleful silence beyond that impermeable partition, there resided a presence of monolithic magnitude, ancient and timeless. It was here that we communed.

Slumbering eons passed as we exchanged excerpts of emotion and experience, intention and desire, not via language or thought but rather an expulsion of impulses traveling along an unseen umbilical tether, adrift in a mingling miasma of amniotic will. We were saturated in awe and jubilant euphoria and quaking terror teetering upon the cusp of transcendence. After time untold this improvised conversation concluded, culminating in a trumpeting question projected of pure intent from beyond the barrier to which I obediently replied affirmatively.

With that affirmation we were thrust back through the limitless tapestry of the cosmos, stripped of our collective awareness as I retraced those throbbing fibers and coalesced once more. As my consciousness solidified my eyes burst open and I took a sharp gasping breath. My woeful body was wracked with unbearable agony. I looked to the Molybdus Articulate with dawning horror to find that it had further expanded and something was forcing its way through.

Protruding from the gaping portal, twisting and yawing impossibly, a translucent mass of dense musculature contorted fantastically, extricating itself further. Shivering pseudopods dripping viscous gray ichor pistoned and pulsated from sucking orifices, extruding tentacular probes with such force that the stonework of the lighthouse cracked beneath their heavy impact.

. . .

THE INCONCEIVABLE ENTITY roiled and rippled, folding in upon itself before unfurling elsewhere from pools of fluid flesh. From yawning superficial ventricles jettisoned plumes of amorphous black fog that warped space around them, creating a null black cloud of distortion that hung around the emerging primordial, as if the very light were bending to its domineering will.

Adrenaline and absolute fear sharpened my senses and I began wrenching against my restraints to discover that the strap around my right wrist had been destroyed by the blast. I could just reach the leather belt on my throat enough to work it loose with my fingertips and by craning my neck I could get to the strap around my upper arm with my mouth. As I bit into the leather my jaw erupted in electric pain, the fractured stumps of my teeth grinding raw, exposed nerve endings against the strap. Screaming around the leather I bore down harder, shaking my head back and forth until the strap came free.

The portal was still expanding to accommodate the gargantuan breadth of the creature's distended corpulence and I shuddered to think what unimaginable demise awaited me should one of those lashing tendrils slither across my skin. With one arm completely unbound I made haste in releasing the others. Dropping to the floor I wailed aloud as the bone fragments inside my ankle crunched, a fresh wave of searing pain rocketing through my leg. I collapsed upon the stone as my vision wavered, unconsciousness threatening to overwhelm me. Attempting to stand was futile. I had lost too much blood and hadn't the strength to do more than drag myself across the floor.

. . .

GIVING the portal a wide berth I made grueling progress across the chamber until I reached the top of the staircase and threw myself over, tumbling down the steel steps and spilling onto the grated floor below. Clutching my ribs and wincing I allowed the pain to abate before hoisting myself upright against the railing of the stairs. Every breath sent piercing anguish radiating through my chest. The ground was littered with the twisted corpses of the Cenobium, blood seeping out from beneath their makeshift masks and dribbling through the metallic floor.

Leaning against the wall beside the machine was Maynard Mathers, eyes raked from the orbital sockets, wordlessly mouthing sweet nothings into the endless night as saliva slid from the foaming corners of his lips. In his hands he clutched the journal to his chest. I paused to consider smashing his head into the wall until his twitching body went still and my hands ran slick with his blood. Instead I ripped the journal from his arms and he began mournfully wailing. This was exactly what he'd worked so diligently for and I would see him experience all of it. I limped away, towards the top of the spiral staircase and as I began my excruciating descent the lighthouse began trembling around me.

Hobbling down one stair at a time, supported against the railing, I proceeded with urgency through floor after floor. I passed through the room with the cot and the congealing puddle of black blood where the knotted cadaver of Abernathy lay unmoving and continued my descent into the neglected kitchenette as the tower quaked violently. A resounding crack echoed from above as the stonework of the lighthouse split and a guttural bellow laced with a chorus of fevered whispers and unhinged babbling laughter penetrated the tattered ruins of my addled mind. There was but one floor below me and time was swiftly running out. I hurriedly limped onward down the stairs.

· · ·

I HAD MADE it a quarter of the way down when the entire lighthouse shuddered and slumped dramatically to one side. The sudden jarring impact threw me from the staircase and I plummeted ten feet before partially crashing into a wooden cask and the ground below. At least one rib fractured upon collision and the breath was ripped from my lungs as I lay there gasping, blood oozing from my deafened ear. I clambered upright and lurched for the door, dragging my crippled foot behind me. Throwing open the door I was met with the transitory glow of predawn morning as a hail of meteoric rubble rained down from far above.

A short way from the lighthouse's island, just peeking over the bluffs, I could make out the bobbing mast of Cliff's ship anchored nearby. Dashing outside as large blocks of stone exploded upon the rocks around me I pushed on, daring not to pause long enough to glance upward. A fist sized chunk of stone struck my left shoulder like the blow of a hammer, glancing my ear. Gritting my teeth I trudged across the island until the ship was in full view. At the foot of the rocky shore there was a small weathered dinghy dragged onto the pebbles. Pushing it onto the water, the waves gently lapping against the hull, I rolled into the boat. There were two oars and I inserted them into the oarlock before rowing away from the island towards the ship using the index finger and thumb of my mangled hand as best as I could manage.

Only once I was aboard the creaking ship did I look back upon the lighthouse, leaning drunkenly to one side. The top half was wholly gone and in its stead a tenebrous nimbus of antimatter devoured the sky, wreathed in a halo of warped reality. Among that rancorous cloud looming malevolently over the town of Port Cairn an entity of galactic proportions swelled and stretched its protracted appendages, lengthened by the dilation of spacetime, exuded from its hyper dimensional presence.

· · ·

THE MENTAL AND cognitive capabilities of my rudimentary cerebral cortex floundered to process the abstruse information into cohesive imagery and the event unfolding before me appeared to transpire through a hyperbolic lens focused on the astronomical mass. As I stared slack-jawed I witnessed the stone of the island, the canopies of the trees, the oceanic waters surrounding the lighthouse elongate and spaghettify, siphoned indiscriminately into the nebulous void emanating from the eldritch entity. The more matter the cloud consumed that much more it expanded in size, dilating exponentially, and the larger the cloud became that much more of the creature emerged from elsewhere.

Unfettered dread dominated my senses. I was ensorcelled with stellar erudition and baffling awe. From the depths of whatever dank chasm it had receded into the stuttering voice of my reason beseeched me with dire urgency to break that paralysis, to abandon this accursed coast and abscond to the sea. Driven by the crazed, fleeting fantasy of self preservation I frantically raised the anchor, lowered the sails, and directed the ship far out into the open ocean waters.

It has been three days since I fled the shores of Port Cairn and I can now see blackness creeping over the horizon. Not once have I raised the sails since my departure and yet the winds have gone silent. When the wind ceased to blow the waves settled into a disquieting stillness. As far as the eye can see there is a glassy black ocean, a sheet of unbroken obsidian that stretches boundlessly undisturbed.

The sun has grown swollen and dim, unmoving in the sky since yesterday morning. The sky itself is now a hazy crimson, ozone deficient distortion of heat waves and electrostatic discharge. There are sores and lesions erupting across my sun baked skin. The wounds I've accrued have turned septic and rampant infection burns in my blood.

. . .

FOR THREE DAYS I've paced and pondered and prayed before resigning myself to the immutable truth and succumbing to the inevitable conclusion. The ship has meager provisions of salted meat and water on board but I must admit, I haven't had much of an appetite since Meredith's sumptuous feast. After the first night I renounced the desire for sleep. I tried but my dreams were fraught with harrowing visions, raving madness and insatiable hunger. I dreamt of collapsing stars and rupturing nuclei and the sweet lulling allure of the Molybdus Articulate. Rather than sleep I've chronicled the events of this last week, documenting my account in the remaining blank pages of Maynard's journal. I am certain there will be no posterity to ever read this and, perhaps, that is for the best. If this serves as nothing more than my confessional then so be it.

THE PRIMORDIAL BARON has risen and I, Edmond Jameson, am responsible for ushering its return from eternal exile.